Clint heard steel clearing leather before Marshal Heck Thomas could react. He released both beers and had his own gun out before one of the mugs hit the floor with a crash. Clint saw three men stand up and draw their guns, about to let lead fly at Heck, who went for his own gun. All five weapons began to belch lead at the same time.

The strangers fired so quickly that their aim was off. Heck dropped into a crouch and returned fire. Clint worked the trigger of his own gun, blowing one of the men almost clean out of his boots with two shots.

The other two were diving for cover, but Thomas's aim was much better than theirs. He hit one man in the chest and the other in the leg. One wounded man went down on his back, saw Clint across the room with his gun drawn, and tried to fire—but Clint was already firing. He drilled the wounded man through the forehead, killing him instantly.

Clint turned to check the room, to make sure no one else was drawing his gun. The bartender, Jasper, had a scatter-gun in his hand to help Clint and Heck, only they'd been too fast and he never got a shot off. When he saw Clint looking at him he dropped the shotgun onto the bar and raised his hands.

"I was just gonna help," he said.

"You can help," Heck said, "by gettin' us another two beers."

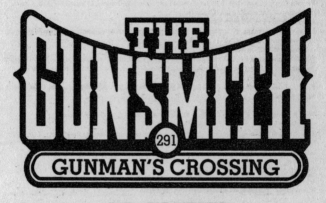

THE GUNSMITH

291

GUNMAN'S CROSSING

J. R. ROBERTS

JOVE BOOKS, NEW YORK

THE BERKLEY PUBLISHING GROUP
Published by the Penguin Group
Penguin Group (USA) Inc.
375 Hudson Street, New York, New York 10014, USA
Penguin Group (Canada), 90 Eglinton Avenue East, Suite 700, Toronto, Ontario M4P 2Y3, Canada
(a division of Pearson Penguin Canada Inc.)
Penguin Books Ltd., 80 Strand, London WC2R 0RL, England
Penguin Group Ireland, 25 St. Stephen's Green, Dublin 2, Ireland (a division of Penguin Books Ltd.)
Penguin Group (Australia), 250 Camberwell Road, Camberwell, Victoria 3124, Australia
(a division of Pearson Australia Group Pty. Ltd.)
Penguin Books India Pvt. Ltd., 11 Community Centre, Panchsheel Park, New Delhi—110 017, India
Penguin Group (NZ), Cnr. Airborne and Rosedale Roads, Albany, Auckland 1310, New Zealand
(a division of Pearson New Zealand Ltd.)
Penguin Books (South Africa) (Pty.) Ltd., 24 Sturdee Avenue, Rosebank, Johannesburg 2196,
South Africa

Penguin Books Ltd., Registered Offices: 80 Strand, London WC2R 0RL, England

This is a work of fiction. Names, characters, places, and incidents either are the product of the author's imagination or are used fictitiously, and any resemblance to actual persons, living or dead, business establishments, events, or locales is entirely coincidental.

GUNMAN'S CROSSING

A Jove Book / published by arrangement with the author

PRINTING HISTORY
Jove edition / March 2006

Copyright © 2006 by Robert J. Randisi.

ISBN: 0-515-14092-9

JOVE®
Jove Books are published by The Berkley Publishing Group,
a division of Penguin Group (USA) Inc.,
375 Hudson Street, New York, New York 10014.
JOVE is a registered trademark of Penguin Group (USA) Inc.
The "J" design is a trademark belonging to Penguin Group (USA) Inc.

PRINTED IN THE UNITED STATES OF AMERICA

10 9 8 7 6 5 4 3 2 1

ONE

The starched white collar made Clint Adams's neck itch, and no amount of adjustments would make it stop. He suspected that Beau Jefferson had insisted on formal dress at this poker game just so the collars would distract his opponents.

Jefferson purported to be the best gambler in Shreveport, Louisiana. He had few nay-sayers in his belief. Clint had never played poker with him before, but a couple of his friends who were present had. He'd had dinner with Bat Masterson and Luke Short the night before the game was to begin, and both had their own opinions.

"Not bad," Luke said. "I've played against him once or twice and he managed to hold his own."

"Have you played against him here?" Clint asked. "In his home town?"

"No," Short said. "Let me think . . . both games were elsewhere. San Francisco, I think, and the other . . . I can't recall."

"Bat?" Clint asked.

"Once," Bat said. "In Denver. I came out second to Beau that night, but that was largely due to luck."

"Your bad," Luke asked, "or his good."

1

"Both, I suppose," Bat said. "I drew three jacks in the last hand of stud, and got my fourth."

"And that was your good luck?" Clint asked.

"Or bad, depending on how you look at it," Bat said. "I was far and away the winner that night when I got that hand. I looked around the table and only Beau was calling me, and he'd drawn three cards."

"I think I can tell where this is going," Clint said.

"I know you do," Bat said. "He held two Aces and drew two more. Pure, dumb luck."

"His or yours?" Luke asked.

Bat made a rude noise with his mouth and said with a wave of his hand, "Take your pick. He took a major portion of my stake that hand. I still managed to comer out a winner, but Beau ended up the big winner."

"Not much you can do about that luck," Clint said.

In fact, there wasn't much you could do about bad luck, and Clint was finding that out. Even the few hands he'd won on this night he'd managed to bluff. The big winners at the table were Luke Short and Beauregard Jefferson. Bat Masterson had managed to play even up to that point. Clint's bluffed hands happened to be big ones, but he was still down a third of his stake. The other three players in the game had busted out long ago, but had remained to watch the four who were left. After all, three of them were among the biggest names in the West, whether it be cards or guns. And three players who were watching were simply a judge, a banker, and a politician. Watching three legends of the West try to take Beau Jefferson's money was a treat.

All three of the men watching were smoking fat stogies, so the air above the table was thick with smoke.

Beau Jefferson was in his early thirties, the son of a wealthy plantation owner who did not appreciate his son's gambling ways. Still, he supplied Beau with money and paid off most of his gambling debts. He loved his son, despite his vices, and agreed to support him as long as he made Shreveport his home. If he ever moved away permanently he would be on his own.

Beau did travel quite a bit, especially if he heard of a big game in Denver or San Francisco or Sacramento, but he seemed to feel that his luck was better when he played in Louisiana—specifically New Orleans, or his home town of Shreveport. And in point of fact, he did play with more confidence, as he had been doing this night.

"Jesus Christ," Luke Short said, at one point, "you fellas tryin' to fix it so we can't see our cards." He fanned with his hand the huge cloud of smoke that hung above the table, trying to dispel it or, at least, get it to move on.

"Sorry," Judge Henry Turnbuckle said. He and the other two observers tried to aid in dispersing the cloud by waving their own hands at it.

"It's up to you, Beau," said Luke Short, who was the dealer of this particular hand. "You were the opener."

Beau studied his cards. He had drawn two. He either had three of a kind or wanted the others to think he had three of a kind. If he had them he'd bet big. If he didn't, he'd still bet, maybe even bigger to convince them. But if he bet timidly, he'd give away his hand as no better than a pair.

"Five hundred."

The stakes were pretty high, and since the last four players had all of the money from the judge, the lawyer and the politician between them, the bets had gone up.

"Pretty goods bet," Luke said. He looked at his own hand, frowned, and then blinked, as if the smoke was still bothering him. "Sonofabitch! I could have a full house in my hand and not know it. I fold."

Clint knew Luke did not have a full house, or he would have bet the hell out of it.

The play moved on to Bat, who studied his cards intently.

"I'll call," he said, then, "and I'll raise a thousand."

"Fifteen hundred to you, Clint," Luke said, still the dealer and in control of the table.

Clint looked at his own cards. He'd been dealt three
fives, a hand that had probably cost him more money over
the years than anything else. Any three of a kind embold-
ened a five card stud player, but three fives, or lower? They
gave too many players false confidence.

But Clint didn't have false confidence. His luck had
been running bad, but he'd won every time he'd bluffed.
He had a decent hand, so this was only a semi-bluff.

"A thousand more," he said.

The judge leaned over and poked the banker in the ribs
with his elbow.

"That's your money he's puttin' in that pot."

"And yours," the banker said. "Don't forget that."

Beau Jefferson looked at Clint, studying him closely.

"I daresay you're bluffin', Mr. Adams," he said. "I do
believe you are."

"Call him, then," Luke Short said.

"I shall," Beau said, "oh, I shall. I call the thousand dollars, and raise two."

They were not playing with chips, but with paper
money. It took some time for Beau to count out the money
for the bet, and the sound of paper against paper filled the
room.

"Bat?" Luke asked. "Three thousand more to you."

"Well, hell," Bat said, "one of 'em ain't bluffin'! I fold."

"And to you, Clint."

Well, Clint had gone in this far, so he had to go all the
way. If he lost this hand he'd be out of the game.

He counted the money in front of him. He had two
thousand one hundred dollars. He separated a hundred dollars from the rest and dropped it into the middle of the
table.

"I call."

Beau stared at him.

"Did you think I wouldn't?"

"I had hoped," Beau said.

"Whataya got, Beau?" Luke asked.

Beau laid his cards on the table. He'd been dealt three fours and had not improved on them.

Clint laid his cards down.

"Three fives," Luke Short said, "beats three fours."

"Every time," Bat said—and Clint noticed that the comment was made a bit smugly.

"Well played, Mr. Adams," Beau said.

"It's getting light out," Luke said, as Clint collected the cards for the next deal. "Shall we continue?"

"Why not?" Beau asked. "At least another hour, anyway. I believe I'm about to get very hot."

"Deal 'em, Clint," Bat said. "I want to see just how hot he gets."

TWO

Beau Jefferson did not get hot.

He got cold.

Very cold.

Clint Adams got hot.

Very hot.

Extremely hot.

The cards suddenly started to come his way. It seemed that in every hand he got just what he needed on the draw. By the end of that hour he had most of the money on the table. Beau Jefferson had busted out, Bat and Luke were collecting what meager stake they still had left.

"That," Bat Masterson said, "was quite an hour."

"And a hell of a display," Luke Short said.

"Hell," Clint said, "I got lucky."

"Yeah, you did," Bat said.

"That's what I meant," Luke said. "A helluva display of luck."

"Gentlemen," Beau Jefferson said, "I'm afraid I must bid you good mornin', and retire with my tail betwixt my legs. I can't remember the last time I was beaten so badly in my own game."

He came around the table to shake Clint's hand, then turned to usher the judge, the banker, and the politician out.

"Breakfast?" Clint asked Bat and Luke.

"On you?" Bat asked.

"Of course, on me."

"Let's eat," Luke said.

They were all staying at different Shreveport hotels, but since Clint was buying they decided to go to the dining room in his.

The Shreveport Manor was not the biggest hotel in the city. That honor went to the Shreveport House, where Bat was staying. Luke had chosen to stay at a small rooming house, where he could keep a low profile.

"There are still some people mad at me about Fort Worth," he told them.

They knew about Luke's trouble in Fort Worth. Hell, they were there with him, at the end when he had been forced to kill Longhaired Jim Courtwright.

The Shreveport Manor may not have been as ostentatious as the Shreveport House, but Clint believed it had one of the best dining rooms in the city.

They were shown to a table by the waiter who had been taking care of Clint since his arrival. Clint had, in turn, been taking care of the waiter, tipping him generously.

"Thank you, Patrick," Clint said.

"Coffee?" Patrick asked.

"Yes," Clint said. "A pot and three cups."

"Comin' up."

"Seems you have the lad trained," Luke said.

"He's a good waiter," Clint said.

"Who else you got trained that well?" Bat asked.

Before he could even answer another young man came hurrying up to the table, saying, "Mr. Adams! There you are."

"Here I am, Jerry," Clint said. "Gents, this is the hotel desk clerk. Jerry, meet Bat Masterson and Luke Short."

The names brought the young man up short.

"Really?"

"Yes," Clint said, "really." He noticed that Jerry was holding a yellow slip of paper. "Is that for me?"

Jerry was staring at Bat and Luke, jerked his eyes back to Clint and said, "Oh, yes. It came in late yesterday, but I haven't seen you since then. It looks like you gents have been out all night."

"Hand it over, then."

Jerry did so and Clint also tipped him generously. The clerk then headed back to his desk, casting glances back over his shoulder at the three men.

"What's the emergency?" Bat asked.

Clint unfolded the telegram and read it. It was brief and to the point, but there was some sense of urgency in it.

"It's from Heck Thomas," Clint said. "Wants me to meet him in Amarillo."

"When?" Luke asked.

"Pronto," Clint said, "if not sooner."

"Trouble?" Bat asked.

"Not spelled out," Clint said, "but it sounds like it." He then read the telegram to them. " *'Need your help. Please meet me in Amarillo pronto.'* "

"Not even long enough for some stops," Luke said.

"What're you gonna do?" Bat asked.

Clint folded the telegram and tucked it into his pocket.

"Guess I'll be going to Amarillo," Clint said. He spotted the waiter coming their way with the coffee. "But that won't be until after I eat breakfast."

"Good," Bat said.

"Yeah," Luke said, "since you're payin'."

THREE

Amarillo was a thriving Texas city, one which oddly enough Clint Adams had been to only once or twice in his life. He'd spent plenty of time in places like Dallas, Fort Worth, San Antonio, Austin, but somehow Amarillo had managed to elude him as a regular stop.

Once he'd safely tucked away his Darley Arabian, Eclipse, in a livery and registered at a hotel he took to the streets. Whenever he found himself in a new place—or re-visited a place he hadn't been in a long time—he liked to walk around and get the feel of it. Amarillo's streets had a pace—and a pulse—he could feel. He wondered what had brought Heck Thomas there. Last he heard Heck was wearing a badge and riding the Indian Territories for Judge Parker, out of Fort Smith. In addition to trying to keep the Five Nations in line, not to mention all of the white men who were killing and stealing in the Oklahoma territories, had Heck Thomas found something else to occupy his time?

Both Bat Masterson and Luke Short had offered—separately, not together—to accompany Clint to Amarillo. They were both acquainted with Heck Thomas and, like Clint, knew him to be a lawman with integrity, and a good

11

man. However, they each had definite plans about where
they were going next, so Clint told them to keep to their
plans. He didn't know what Heck wanted, but if it turned
out to be something he couldn't help him with, he'd let
them know. He thanked them each in turn, as he knew that
it was more out of friendship for him that they were making their offers.

The part of the telegram he hadn't read to Bat and Luke
had mentioned a place called The Black Rose Cantina.
Heck had said he would be there at a certain time for three
days. There was no mention about what he'd do if Clint
could not make it during that three day window. In point of
fact, Clint was there on day two, so finding Heck Thomas
should not prove to be a problem.

Clint took his look at the town, stopped to have a beer
along the way once or twice, had a bath, then went back to
his hotel to change out of his dirty trail clothes.

While dressing he thought back to his last night in
Shreveport, Louisiana . . .

He had met Miss Alicia DuBois his first night in Shreveport. A tall, high-breasted, statuesque beauty, her eyes had
found him across the floor of a local casino and, during the
course of the evening, they managed to draw closer and
closer to each other, until finally they were standing side
by side.

Clint knew they had exchanged words, but he didn't remember what they were. All he remembered was that a
short time later they were in his room, in his bed. He spent
another two nights with her, and the morning he returned to
his room with Heck Thomas's telegram in his pocket, she
was waiting there for him . . .

As he walked in he saw her lying there with the white sheet
molded to her. She was tall, long-legged, with full breasts
and wide hips. The sheet was like a second skin on her, and

he could see the outline of her nipples. Her black hair was fanned out on the pillow around her head.

"Good morning," she greeted him. "Did you win?"

"Of course."

She stretched, then, luxuriously and he watched what it made her body do beneath the sheet.

"Why don't you look happy, then?" she asked. "You won, and you have a beautiful-named woman waiting for you in your bed. What could be better?"

He smiled, took the telegram from his pocket.

"I guess it would have been better if I hadn't gotten this."

He explained to her what was in the telegram, and that he had to leave immediately.

"Without sleep?" she asked.

"Yes."

"Without breakfast?"

"I had breakfast with Bat and Luke."

She took hold of the sheet with one hand and tossed it back. Not only was she naked, she was probably—in that moment—the most naked-looking woman he'd ever seen.

"Without saying goodbye?"

"That," he said, "I would never do."

FOUR

He undressed while she watched, and as soon as his erect penis came into view she was on him. She grasped him firmly and pulled him to the bed. As he stood there she stroked the length of him with one hand, and fondled his testicles with the other. Then she leaned in and began to kiss his belly. Clint felt a moan building up inside of him, and then he couldn't hold it any longer.

"Jesus," he said, as her hot mouth moved lower, her tongue leaving a wet trail behind.

She actually pushed him away from the bed then, so she could sink to her knees in front of him. She slid her hands around so she was cupping his buttocks and, holding him that way, engulfed him with her mouth.

She began to suck him wetly, sliding her head up and down, at times actually slurping, as if he was the most delicious thing she had ever had in her mouth. The sounds she made increased his own ardor and he felt himself swelling within her mouth.

Alicia suckled him until he was almost bursting, then released him from her mouth. She got to her feet and kissed him, her full breasts crushed against his chest, his penis trapped between them. She kissed him avidly as he

15

put his arms around her, then slid his hands down the line of her back until it was he who was cupping her buttocks.

He walked her back the few feet to the bed so that the mattress struck the back of her legs. He pushed and she had no choice but to fall back on it. Climbing onto the bed with her he powered his mouth to her nipples and sucked them, making them very wet and distended. They were dark brown, the aureola very wide. They were heavy breasts, and they slid to one side as she lay on her back. He used his hands to push them together so he could ravish them at the same time. She groaned, reached for him, but he quickly pushed her hands away. He began to kiss his way down her body until he was nestled in the dark forest between her legs. His tongue found her wet, hot and waiting and he lapped up her sweetness, making her squirm beneath him. He pinned her thighs beneath his arms, continued to kiss and suck on her until she was moaning and crying out. The sensations caused by his lips and tongue were so intense she wanted to move, but he wouldn't let her. Finally, as waves of orgasm overcame her, she began beating at him with her fists to get away from him. She thought that if he didn't stop she'd die, but at the same time if he did stop she'd die.

At last he released her, allowing her to move about on the bed so that her back was pressed against the bedpost.

"Wait," she said, panting, holding a hand out to him, "wait . . ."

"I can't," he told her. "I want you now."

"You're killing me," she said. "I have to catch my breath."

He looked down at his rigid penis, which was huge.

"Does this look like I can wait?"

She stared at him, saw that his cock was prodding the air, as if it was trying to get at her.

"God," she said, "you're so beautiful. Has anyone ever told you that?"

Women had said that about his penis before, and it embarrassed him. He never knew what to say.

"I want to be inside you," he said.

"You can't," she said. "You've made me too sensitive there, with your mouth. If you put that inside of me now, I'll die."

"Alicia—"

"Lie on your back," she said, reaching out to him. "Lie down. You won't be sorry. I promise."

They'd spent several nights together already—and some mornings—so he knew she was telling the truth. He turned and settled down onto his back, his head on a pillow. Her hands were on him immediately, rubbing his chest, his abdomen. She leaned over him, kissed his neck, his chest, brushed his skin with her nipples. She slid down his body until his penis was between her breasts. She used her hands to press her breasts together, trapping him there, and then began to move on him, sliding his penis up and down, fucking him with her tits.

If Clint had had the ability to think at that moment he might have wondered if a woman had ever done this to him before. But he couldn't think, all he could do was feel. He was trapped there between her bosoms, her skin gliding up and down him, and every so often she'd duck her head down and lick the tip of him.

"Do you like this?" she asked him.

"I love it," he said, truthfully.

Abruptly, she stopped.

"What—" he said.

"It's time," she said, sliding up him. "I have to have you inside me now."

She straddled him, reached between them to grasp him and guide him to her, and then inside of her. She lifted her hips and brought herself down on him, taking him inside the steaming depths of her. She rode him that way, her head back, her breasts thrust out, bucking on him as he grabbed and squeezed her tits, pinched her nipples, tried to stay with her. Her breath began to come in harsh gasps. She pressed her hands down on his abdomen and began to lift herself higher, until he almost slid out of her, and then dropped down on him roughly, twisting at the same time.

The ride went on for some time, his own gasps and groans mixing with hers, until finally he exploded inside her . . . and he was anything—everything—but sorry, as she had promised.

FIVE

After that energetic session in bed with Alicia DuBois Clint forced himself to get dressed and leave. She watched him from the bed. A bemused look on her face.

"Will you come back?" she asked.

"Probably," he said. "Some day. If you promise to do that . . . thing you did with your breasts again. I've never experienced that before."

"I've taught that to my girls," she said. "Men seem to like it."

"Yes," he said, "I can see why they would."

He kissed Madam Alicia—as she was called when she was working—goodbye, saddled Eclipse and headed for Amarillo . . .

Clint found his way to The Black Rose Cantina, although it wasn't easy. It wasn't on any main street. Hell, it was hardly even on a side street, but more like an alley. He had to ask directions of three different people before he finally found it.

Yet, even with all that trouble, he was the first to arrive. Heck Thomas was nowhere to be seen, so Clint took himself to the bar for a beer.

For a place as well hidden as The Black Rose, it was a remarkably clean and cheerful place. The bar top was relatively clean, the bartender cheerful, and saloon girls attentive—two dark-eyed, black-haired senoritas tried to lure Clint to a back room even before he got to the bar— and the customers were remarkably willing to ignore him and mind their own business. The drank, ate, conversed, and never gave him a second look. That was odd for any saloon.

"What can I getcha?" the barman asked.

"Beer any good?"

"Best in Amarillo."

"Then I'll take one."

The bartender drew the beer and plunked the frosty mug down in front of Clint.

"You Adams?"

Clint paused over his mug, then took the time to have a sip before answering.

"Who wants to know?"

"Heck Thomas."

"Where is he?"

"In the back."

Clint looked toward the back of the room.

"There's a private room back there."

Clint looked back at the man.

"You are Adams, right?"

"How'd you know?"

"Only regulars come in here."

"Heck a regular?"

"When he's in town," the man said. "That's regular enough."

"Is he okay?"

"He's fine. He's just bein' careful. You can go on back."

"I would," Clint said, "except I'm kind of careful myself."

"I getcha."

He waved to one of the girls to come over.

"You change your mind, handsome?" she asked. She was short, and pressed her plump breasts against Clint's side. He looked right down her cleavage. On another day . . .

"Forget it, Carmen," the man said. "Go back and tell Marshal Thomas that Clint Adams is here."

"Ah, so that's who you are, eh?" she asked. She rubbed herself against him and he could feel her large nipples through the material of her blouse and his shirt—and she knew it.

"That's who I am."

"Maybe we can get acquainted later?"

What could he say?

"Maybe."

"I get *el jefe* for you. You wait right here."

"Where else would I go?"

He watched as she flounced across the room, attracting the attention of all the men in the place. They had managed to ignore a stranger in their midst, but a pretty girl could not go unnoticed.

As he watched her Clint wondered just how much of a stranger he really was. If the bartender was expecting him, how many of these men were—and how many of them guessed who he was when he came through the front door?

She reached a door in the back wall, knocked and entered. Clint hadn't really suspected a trap, but he always thought it was better to be safe than dead. He kept his eye on the door while working on his beer, and at the same time stayed aware of what was going on around him. Admittedly, it wasn't much, but the last thing he needed was some fella who seemed disinterested all of a sudden going for his gun. It had happened before.

He looked at the bartender and asked, "What's your name?"

"Jasper."

"How long has Heck been here today, Jasper?"

"Today?" the bartender said. "Hell, he's been here for days. Here, you better take this."

He drew two more cold beers and put them in front of Clint.

"He's gonna want one," Jasper said.

"Is he drunk?" Clint asked.

"Well, if he ain't I'm gonna be real surprised."

Clint turned and looked at the door again just as it opened and Carmen came out. She smiled and waved to Clint, but he didn't move until he saw Heck Thomas fill the doorway behind her.

He left his half-finished beer on the bar, picked up the two fresh ones and started for the back of the room. Two seconds later he knew he'd made a bad mistake.

SIX

Clint heard steel clearing leather before he even saw Heck Thomas reacting. He released both beers and had his own gun out before one of the mugs hit the floor with a crash.

Chairs scraped the floor as patrons of the saloon dove for cover. Clint saw that three men had stood up, drew their guns and were about to let lead fly at Heck.

Heck Thomas, seeing the three men stand up, knew what was coming and went for his own gun. All five weapons began to belch lead and death at the same time.

Chunks of wood were gouged from the doorway around Heck, as well as the door behind him which was partially open. The men had fired so quickly that their aim was off. Heck dropped into a crouch and returned fire.

Clint worked the trigger of his own gun, blowing one of the men almost clean out of his boots with two shots. He'd meant the second shot for one of the other men, but they had begun to move themselves, and the same man ducked into the second bullet right after the first one hit him.

The other two were diving for cover as Heck returned fire, but the marshal's aim was much better than theirs. He hit one man in the chest and the other in the leg. The wounded man went down on his back, saw Clint across the

23

room with his gun drawn, and tried to fire at him, but Clint
was already firing. He drilled the wounded man right
through the forehead, killing him instantly, and suddenly
the room was quiet.

Clint turned to check the room, to make sure no one else
was drawing their gun. The bartender, Jasper, had a scatter-
gun in his hand, but he had gone for it to help Clint and
Heck, only they'd been too fast for him and he never got a
shot off. When he saw Clint looking at him he dropped the
shotgun onto the bar and raised his hands.

"I was just gonna help," he said.

"You can help," Heck said, from across the room, "by
gettin' us another two beers."

"Sure thing, Heck."

"Bring 'em back here, Jasper."

"Sure."

"What about these three?" Clint asked.

"I expect the local law will be along soon," Heck said.
"Let's see if we can't finish our conversation before that
happens. Jasper?"

"Yeah, Marshal?"

"Send the law back when they get here."

"Yes, sir."

"Clint?"

Heck walked to the open doorway, ejecting spent shells
from his gun as he went. Clint had already done so and re-
loaded, and now he watched his friend's back until they
were in the room with the door closed.

"Pull up a barrel," Heck said.

There was a small desk and a chair back there, but nothing else except supplies.

"What was that all about, Heck?"

"You know what it's like to be a target, Clint."

Clint studied his friend. Tall and handsome, there were
some lines on his face that came from worry, not from age,
because Heck Thomas was not yet forty. His big mustache,

which virtually hid his mouth, had some gray in it, otherwise he looked about the same as the last time Clint had
seen him some years ago.

"What are you doing in Texas?", Clint asked. "I heard
you were wearing a badge, running down bad men in the
Five Nations for Judge Parker."

Heck pushed aside the lapel of the jacket he was wearing to show Clint his badge.

"Still am," he said. "I got special dispensation from the
judge to be here."

"Doing what?"

"I'm huntin' down the Frank Sunday gang."

"Frank Sunday," Clint said. "I guess I've never heard of
him."

"He and his men have been killin' white men and Indi-
ans alike, women and children and all on the Territories."

"And now they're outside the Territories," Clint said.
"Why are they still your business?"

Heck leaned forward and Clint could see how bloodshot
his eyes were.

"I'm makin' it my business!" he said, fiercely.

At that moment the door opened and Jasper stepped in
with two beers. The bartender could feel the tension in the
air so he just handed each man a beer and took his leave,
closing the door behind him.

"I want these boys, Clint," Heck said. "I want them
bad."

"Are you tracking them alone, Heck?"

"That's right," the man said. He drank some beer, wiped
off his mustache with his hand. "None of the other mar-
shals wanted to come with me."

"Why didn't the judge make one or more of them go
with you?"

"Because he don't want the gang as much as I do, either," Heck explained. "He's satisfied when them leavin'
his jurisdiction."

"And you're not?"

"Hell no!" Heck almost exploded. "I seen too much of the killin' they did, Clint. I seen children they killed and scalped."

"Indian children?"

"Does it matter?"

Actually, it didn't, Clint felt bad for having asked the question.

"What do you want me to do, Heck?"

"You saw what happened out there," Heck said. "Sunday's got lots of men willin' to watch his back, tryin' to stop me from trackin' him. Me, I got nobody willin' to watch mine."

Clint stood up off the barrel he'd been perched on and said, "Well, you got somebody now, Heck. If that's what you want from me, you got it."

"You already done it once today," Heck said, "better than anybody else coulda. I just want you to keep me alive long enough to track those sumbitches down."

Clint approached his friend and they clinked beer mugs.

"You got it," he said, again.

SEVEN

They would have liked to leave right away but it wasn't to be. As Heck had predicted the local law showed up to look into the shooting, and have the bodies removed.

"I don't know these three boys," Sheriff Hal Jordan said. "If I did I think you boys would be in trouble."

"This badge says different, Sheriff," Heck said.

"That badge may make you somebody in the Nations, Marshal, but it don't make you nobody here."

"You've got plenty of witnesses who saw what happened, Sheriff," Clint said. "It was all clear self defense."

"Yeah, you're right," Jordan said. "I do have witnesses— and I got three dead men. I don't want any more."

They were all seated in the sheriff's office and it was already dusk out. Too late for Clint and Heck to hit the trail.

"I want you boys out of town by first light," the sheriff said. "And take with you whatever trouble you're trailin', or is trailin' you."

Heck stood up and said, "That's our plan, Sheriff."

"I suggest you find a hotel for the night and hole up," Jordan said, as Clint stood. "Fellas with reputations like yours just invite trouble."

"We're gonna get a meal, Sheriff," Heck said. "Just like any other law abidin' citizen would."

"And then we'll go to our hotel," Clint assured the man. "We're not looking for trouble, Sheriff."

"Good," Jordan said, "because I'd hate to have to try and take your guns away."

Heck stiffened and said, "We'd hate to see that too, Sheriff."

"Like I said, you got reputations," Jordan went on. "I know who you are, but I been wearin' a badge for over twenty years and I ain't never backed down from no man."

"We can appreciate that, Sheriff," Clint said, trying to diffuse the situation. Heck Thomas was under a strain, and he was ready to explode, but the local lawman was the wrong target. "There won't be any more trouble from us . . ."

"Good."

". . . as long as we have other choices."

The sheriff sighed, then said, "Okay, fine."

"We can go?" Clint asked.

"Yeah," Jordan said, "the witness statements and the fact that the marshal here does have a badge—even if he's out of his jurisdiction—means I've got nothin' to hold you over for."

"Judge Parker will appreciate this, Sheriff," Clint said.

"Hangin' Judge Parker?" Jordan asked.

"That's who the marshal rides for."

Jordan shook his head. He didn't need another big reputation being brought into play.

"Just go," he said.

Clint grabbed Heck's arm and pulled him toward the door.

"I know, I know," Heck said, once they were outside. "He's just doin' his job."

"That's right," Clint said, "and technically speaking, even though you've got a badge and Judge Parker's permission to leave the Territories, this isn't your job. This is something you feel you have to do. You've made it personal, Heck."

Heck Thomas frowned.

"I never did that before, Clint," he said. "Maybe I've been wearin' a badge too long."

"Maybe you're just mad, Heck," Clint said. "Every once in a while we're entitled to just get mad, aren't we?"

"I guess we are."

"You got a room in a hotel?"

"No," Heck said, "I was just sleepin' in the back room of The Black Rose."

"Well, come on," Clint said. "We'll get you a room at my hotel, and then we'll get a steak."

"Sounds good to me," Heck said.

EIGHT

Clint and Heck had their steaks and then did what they told the sheriff they were going to do, went to their hotel rooms.

"Get a good night's sleep, Heck," Clint said. "I don't think anybody else'll be trying anything, tonight."

"I'll set up some warnin' systems in my room, anyway," Heck Thomas said.

Clint knew what Heck meant. Many was the time he went to sleep with a pitcher by the door and a basin on the windowsill, where anyone trying to sneak into the room would knock them over and make a helluva racket. Heck's room was right across from his, so he knew he'd hear it, too.

Clint went to his own room and busied himself cleaning his rifle and his pistols. Chances were he and Heck would be on the trail of the Sunday gang for weeks. He wanted to make sure his weapons were in proper working order.

Over dinner Heck had filled Clint in on Frank Sunday. The man was in his late thirties, had been riding with different gangs over the years before he finally formed his own—and he had collected as vicious a bunch of owlhoots as he could find. There were none as vicious as he himself,

31

though. Sunday liked to kill. He didn't just get a thrill out of it, he needed to do it, and the more brutal the better he liked it.

Clint had known men like that before, men who deserved to be killed. In fact, he'd killed quite a few of them himself. He'd taken no pleasure from any of them, but he had taken some satisfaction that they would not be hurting or killing anyone else.

When he'd finished cleaning his weapons he started to get restless. Normally, he would have gone to a saloon for a beer, maybe found a poker game. He had a copy of the Victor Hugo novel *Lucretia Borgia* in his saddlebags. It was a favorite of Buffalo Bill Cody's—in fact, he'd named his big fifty rifle after it—and Clint had always meant to read it. He dug it out, kicked his boots off, hung his gunbelt on the bedpost and sat on the bed to do just that. But he had only read a few pages when there was a knock at his door.

He put the book down, stood up, slid his gun from his holster and went to answer it. He'd done this very same thing hundreds of times before in hundreds of hotel rooms in hundreds of towns and never knew what was on the other side of the door.

When he opened it and found the plump saloon girl from the cantina, Carmen, standing there he relaxed, but just a bit.

"Hello, Carmen."

She smiled at him. She had a black shawl tightly around her shoulders, but it did nothing to hide that plump cleavage he'd found so interesting earlier. He found it no less interesting now and, in fact, was finding it hard to keep his eyes off of it. Her skin was creamy and clear, and she looked so healthy, as if she was going to burst from it.

"Can I come in?"

"Well, I don't know," he said. "Aren't you afraid of what it might do to your reputation?"

"That would not be a problem," she said. "I don't have a very good reputation, as it is."

"Well then," he said, "I suppose you better come in, then."

He allowed her to slip past him, which she wasn't able to do without pressing her breasts against him. He took a moment to check the hall, found it empty, and then closed the door and locked it behind them.

"Are you going to shoot me?" she asked.

Of all those hundreds of times he'd answered the door with a gun in his hand he'd actually had to shoot someone several times, but there were other times—most of the times—when it hadn't been necessary. And there were quite a few times when his visitor was a woman.

"No," he said, "I don't think I'll have to do that."

He walked to the bedpost to holster the gun. She walked to the bed and picked the book up from the pillow.

"Victor Hugo," she said. "I am impressed."

"You've read him?"

"I have," she said. "In fact, I read this." She held the book to her breasts, and her black shawl fluttered to the floor, where she left it. "Do you find it unusual that a Mexican saloon girl in a Texas town has read Victor Hugo?"

"I'm constantly surprised where I find culture, Carmen."

"I've read Mark Twain, too," she said. She put the book back down on the pillow, then ran her palm over the white sheet. Leaning over slightly, she was giving him an even better view of her bosom.

"And Robert Louis Stevenson?" he asked.

"Yes."

"Then we have a lot in common."

"I thought that as soon as we met," she confided.

"Have you finished work for the evening?" he asked.

"I have," she said. "In fact, I left early so I could come over here. You don't mind that I came, do you?"

"Of course not," he said. "Why would I mind. We never would have gotten to talk about popular literature otherwise."

"Well," she said, reaching behind her, "I did have something else in mind when I came."

He almost gasped when her dress dropped to the floor and she stood before him gloriously and bodaciously naked.

NINE

Clint's first reaction was to get all of his clothes off. Carmen's body was every bit as delicious-looking as he'd thought it would be. Her breasts were plump and firm, with large, dark nipples. She was short, only about five foot one. Her thighs were almost chunky, her ass full and rounded. She was every inch what a woman should be in bed, pillowy and smooth.

Clint walked around to her side of the bed and sat on it. He reached for her and drew her close, nuzzling those wonderous breasts. He pressed his face between them while he reached behind her to cup her impossibly firm buttocks. He sucked one nipple into his mouth and then the other as she cradled his head to her and moaned.

She reached between them and encountered his rigid penis. Smiling, she slid into his lap so that his cock was between her thighs. She reached down and began to stroke it with her small hands, wrapping her fingers around it. As it jutted up from between her legs it looked oddly as if it were hers—and, in a way, it was. It was all hers. He gave himself up to the sensations as she stroked and fondled him. She put her hands around his neck and started rubbing herself against him. The tangle of pubic hair between her legs did exquisite things to him as she continued to rub up against him. Then, abruptly, he slid his hands beneath her buttocks, lifted her and impaled her on his stiff cock. Her eyes widened and she gasped as he entered her. With her fingers locked behind his neck she began to bounce up and down on his lap. Every time she came down on him he felt as if he was piercing her deeper and deeper. She gasped and moaned and cried out with every bounce and then just as abruptly as he'd lifted her up onto him she slid off his lap and went to her knees in front of him. His penis was shiny with her wetness and she took it into her mouth and began to suck it furiously. She braced herself with her hands on his thighs as her head bobbed up and down on him avidly. He rubbed her back, reached between them to pinch her nipples and squeeze her breasts, but then he couldn't take it anymore. He touched her head to get her to release him from her hot mouth, but she refused. She moaned her objection as he tried to get free of her and finally he had to take a hand full of her long black hair and yank her off of him.

She was on him like a wildcat. She stood up, put both hands against his chest and pushed him down on his back. Next she climbed up on him and sat on his chest, her fragrant mound tantalizingly close to his mouth. Then, with one quick, convulsive movement she pressed her wet vulva to his mouth. With his nose buried in her pubic bush he began to lap at her avidly, licking her, sucking on her as she pressed herself more rightly to his face. For a moment he couldn't breathe and he couldn't think of a better, sweeter way to suffocate but then she moved, allowing some air in through his nose. He reached behind her to press her tightly to his mouth again and slid his tongue in and out of her a few times before sliding it up her wet slit to find her rigid little clit. When he touched it with his tongue she gasped and shuddered and when he flicked it, back and

forth, then up and down, it happened again. Waves of pleasure shot through her body and he could feel her quivering.

With an animal growl she slid down his chest to straddle
his crotch, pinning his penis beneath her, but not allowing
him to enter her.

"Not yet," she gasped, "not yet," and began to run herself wetly up and down his length.

He pulled her down on him so that her breasts were
pressing against him and she continued to rub herself on
him, wetting him thoroughly. Finally, she lifted her hips,
pressed herself against his tip and then slowly took him inside. She leaned over to kiss him, sliding her tongue into
his mouth, then over his lips. They kissed wetly for a long
time as she rode him. The air filled with the sound of wet
flesh against flesh, of even wetter kisses. They were sounds
he enjoyed, that drove him on, that excited him. Suddenly,
he flipped her over onto her back, grabbed hold of each an-
kle and split her apart, driving into her that way. She
grabbed hold of the sheets on either side of her and
whipped her head from side to side as he pounded into her.
He watched her breasts undulate each time he slammed
into her and found the sight fascinating. He continued to
watch until he couldn't hold back any further. He exploded
inside of her as she began to writhe and buck beneath him
and they shared one of the most exquisite moments a man
and woman can experience . . .

Later he woke to find her sleeping on her belly. The bed
sheet had fallen to the floor during their wild lovemaking,
so she was completely naked, snoring just slightly. He
leaned over her and began to plant kisses along the line of
her back. She groaned as he reached the small of her back.
He kissed the dimple just above her buttocks, then got
down between her legs, spreading them so he could lie
there. He kissed her butt cheek, marveling at the smooth-

ness of her skin. He spread them and touched her with his tongue and she came fully awake. He continued to lick her and she ground her butt back into his face, groaning and crying out.

Then she got to her knees and said, "Like this, oh please, like this . . ."

Clint got to his knees behind her, took hold of her butt cheeks and spread them. He'd wet her thoroughly with his tongue so when he pressed the tip of his penis against her he was able to slide in wetly. He continued, inserting himself inch by inch slowly, in case she complained of pain, but she never did, and when he was fully inside of her she began to buck wildly back against him. Any worry he had about hurting her flew out the window and he grabbed her hips and began to move with her. He knew a lot of women didn't like it this way, but Carmen appeared to be one who loved it. She was tight around him as he moved in and out. His penis still felt sensitive from before and it didn't take long before he was spurting again as she tensed around him, holding him tightly as if she was never going to release him . . .

In the morning the sunlight shone through the window onto Carmen's sleeping form and seemed to make her skin glow. They had awakened and made love two more times during the night, and each time she seemed to want it more and more.

As he laid beside her watching her he found himself almost hoping she wouldn't wake up. He was afraid she'd want more, and he wasn't sure he had any more to give— even if he wanted to, which he knew he would. Even watching her lying there on her side with her irresistible butt facing him he felt a stirring that amazed him. If he stayed in this town one more day with this energetic, vital young woman he was sure he'd have a heart attack.

Slowly, he started to get out of bed, trying not to wake

her. She was younger than he was and then some, but he
was sure she could use her sleep. He started to dress and it
was only when he had to remove his gun belt from the bed
post that he thought she'd come awake. Finally, he pulled
on his boots and collected his saddlebags, then looked
back at her. She'd rolled over onto her back and the sight
of her was almost enough to pull him back to the bed. He
knew that if he even leaned over to kiss her goodbye he'd
end up back in bed with her, trying to fuck himself to
death.

He was almost out the door when she spoke from the bed.

"You ever get back this way you better come and see
me, Clint Adams."

"Count on it," he said, and left.

TEN

Clint banged on Heck Thomas's door until the marshal answered it and looked at him bleary-eyed.

"Well, come on," he said to his friend. "It's time for breakfast. What's the matter, not enough sleep?"

"Who could sleep with all the racket you were makin'?" Heck demanded. "This thing with you and women, it hasn't changed, has it?"

"If you're talking about them liking me and me liking them then no, it hasn't," Clint answered, "and I hope it never will. Now are you ready for breakfast or not?"

"I'm ready," Heck said. "I'm comin'."

He went back into the room then reappeared at the door with his rifle and saddlebags. They went down to the hotel dining room and ordered breakfast.

"How's your horse?" Clint asked. "A good one?"

"Yeah," Heck said, "he'll make the trip. You still ridin' that fancy one P.T. Barnum gave ya?"

"The Darley Arabian, yeah," Clint said. "Eclipse."

"Now, that big black gelding you used ta have," Heck said. "That was a horse."

"Duke."

"Yeah," Heck said. "Whatever happened to him?"

"Put him out to pasture," Clint said. "He was getting old, deserved a rest."

"This one any good?"

"Yeah," Clint said, "Eclipse will make the trip."

Over breakfast Heck explained to Clint how he'd been tracking the gang for weeks, from the territories to there in Texas.

"Are they leaving a clear trail?"

"Clear as blood," Heck said. "They ain't hard to track 'cause there's a trail of blood and bodies behind them."

"Where do you figure they're headed?"

"Can't figure," Heck said. "Looks like they're just headin' farther West."

"Tell me more about them," Clint said. "How many?"

"Sunday's got six ridin' with him," Heck said. "His *segundo* is a fella named Arch Jackson. Ever heard of him?"

"No,"

"Mean sonofabitch," Heck said.

"And the others?"

"He's always got two or three he can throw away," Heck said, "like those three last night. But he's also got a couple more been ridin' with him as long as Arch. Ben Dempsey and Will Matson."

"Don't know either of those, either," Clint said. "I must be out of the loop, Heck."

"No reason you should be in it," the lawman said. "You ain't worn a badge in a long time. Wish I could do what you do, Clint."

"What's that?"

"Wander around, play poker, help people who need help," Heck said. "All without the benefit of a badge."

"Badge gets heavy after a while," Clint said.

"Tell me about it," Heck said. "This one's gettin' heavier by the minute."

"Why do you keep wearin' it then?"

Heck reached under his jacket to finger the tin star.

"I guess because the judge pinned it on me," Heck said. "I respect him, Clint, and he respects me. He gave me this badge. I can't just take it off when the goin' gets tough."

"No," Clint said, "I guess not, Heck."

"I aim to bring those men back to the Nations, Clint," Heck said, "or kill them if they resist. You got to understand that."

"I understand one thing, Heck."

"What's that?"

"You need someone to watch your back and make sure you come back alive. I aim to do whatever it takes to make that happen."

ELEVEN

Frank Sunday woke and removed his hat from his eyes. He squinted at the sun, then rolled over and got to his feet. He could feel bones creaking as he stretched. The welcome smell of coffee wafted over to him. There was a story going around that he once killed one of his men because, as last one on watch, he was supposed to make a fresh pot of coffee and didn't. It wasn't a true story and, in fact, had been started by Sunday, himself, but he did need fresh coffee to start out his day in a good mood.

The only thing that put him in as good a mood as good coffee, was a good killing.

He surveyed the camp, saw that he was the first to rise. Over at the fire he saw Arch Jackson crouched down, pouring out a cup of coffee. As he walked to the fire Arch reached behind him without looking and handed Sunday the cup.

"Thanks."

Arch nodded and poured another cup for himself. Sunday moved to the other side of the fire and crouched down.

"You didn't have the last watch," he said to Arch.

"Couldn't sleep, decided to stay up instead of waking Alby for his watch."

Arch was the same age as Sunday, roughly thirty-seven or -eight. Where Sunday was a hard-looking man, with high cheekbones, a strong jaw and a muscular body, Arch Jackson was just mean-looking. He had sloping shoulders, big hands, feral eyes. About the same height, Arch outweighed the strapping Sunday by forty pounds. They were a scary pair when they walked together, and Arch was possibly the strongest man Sunday had ever known, even though he didn't have the defined muscles Sunday did. He was thick through the middle, and a lot of his power came from there. But the thing that Sunday really liked about Arch Jackson was that he was very content to be number two.

Sunday and Arch had been in the same gang for a few years, and when Sunday broke off to start his own, Arch just went with him. They'd never even discussed it. They'd just saddled up one day and rode out together.

That had been two years ago, and they had raised a lot of hell during that time.

"Be out of Texas by midday."

"Good."

"Want me to wake the boys?" Arch asked.

"In a few minutes," Sunday said.

There was a few moments of silence, then Arch asked, "You think he's out there? On our trail?"

"Oh yeah," Sunday said, "he's out there."

"His badge don't mean nothin' once he leaves the Territories."

"It ain't his badge that's trackin' us, Arch," Sunday said. "It's his gun."

"Think those boys we left in Amarillo stopped him?"

"I doubt it. They wasn't much."

"Why'd we leave them there, then?"

"Just keepin' the good marshal on his toes, is all," Sunday said. "We want him to be sharp when he catches up to us."

"What about help? Think he's got any?"

"If he does it ain't anybody from Judge Parker's court," Sunday commented.

"Could be he's got friends."

"Could be."

"Famous friends."

"With big names and reputations."

The two men grinned at each other across the fire. They raised their cups to each other and Sunday said, "The bigger the better."

"Amen."

Reputations meant a lot to Frank Sunday and Arch Jackson. Killing Marshal Heck Thomas and any famous friend he brought along would go a long way towards increasing their reps.

As Arch went around kicking the men awake Sunday poured himself another cup of coffee. He didn't care if Heck Thomas had a posse with him.

Where they were going it wouldn't make much difference.

"You got any idea at all where these boys may be headed?" Clint asked.

They were at the livery, saddling their horses.

"If I did I'd try to get there ahead of them," Heck said. "We're just gonna have to keep trailin' 'em."

Clint finished cinching in Eclipse's saddle and led the horse over to where Heck was pulling the cinch tight on his.

"It ever occur to you that they may be leaving a clear trail for you to follow on purpose?"

"Well, hell, yeah," Heck said. He turned to face Clint. "They know I'm comin', Clint. Frank and I know each other."

"Then he'll know you sent for help."

"And he won't care none," Heck said. "Killin' whoever I bring with me will just be another feather in his cap."

Clint frowned and as they walked their horse outside to mount up he said, "First time I've ever been invited to be a feather in somebody's cap."

TWELVE

Aside from the trail of bodies and rivers of blood the Sunday gang were leaving behind Heck Thomas took the time to show Clint the tracks he'd been following. Heck was a much better tracker than Clint would ever be.

"This horse here favors his foreleg, but he ain't lame. See it? He just doesn't put as much weight down on it as he does his others."

"I see it," Clint said. "That's odd."

"Sure is," Heck said. "You'd think a feller on the run wouldn't want to leave tracks like that. And this one here. See? Needs a new shoe there."

Clint nodded. Heck was right, the gang was leaving a trail clear as day.

"They're taking you somewhere, Heck," Clint said.

Heck stood up and faced Clint.

"You can throw in your hand, Clint, no hard feelings," he said. "I ain't tryin' to pull a fast one on you. These are killers I'm after."

"I know it," Clint said. "That's why I'm here. Don't worry, Heck. I'll see this through."

"I figured you would," the marshal said. "Thanks."

"We better mount up and keep moving."

"These tracks are days old," Heck said.

"They're not moving so fast."

"Naw, they ain't in a hurry," Heck said. "They hit a small town just east of Amarillo. Took the bank, burned the town to the ground. That kinda thing takes time. No, they ain't in no hurry."

"What's the next town?" Clint asked.

"Vega," Heck said. "Small place. I don't see no smoke, so maybe they bypassed it."

"Law there?"

"I think," Heck said. "Might as well check and see."

When they rode into Vega, Texas, it did not show any signs of having fallen victim to the Sunday gang. Buildings were still standing, although there weren't a lot of them. They found their way to the sheriff's office and dismounted there. They had no intention of staying any longer than it took to talk to the man.

As they entered the office a man seated behind a pitted and scarred desk looked up. He was bald, heavy, made no effort to stand up. Clint wondered when the last time was the man had ever tried to sit a horse.

"You the sheriff?" Heck asked.

"That's right," the man said. "Mel Cooley. What can I do for you gents?"

"My name's Marshal Heck Thomas," Heck said. "Ridin' outta Judge Parker's court."

"You're a little far afield, ain'tcha, Marshal?"

"That's right, I am," Heck said. "I'm trackin' a gang led by a man named Frank Sunday. Know 'em?"

The man sat back. His chair creaked in protest. Beads of sweat had suddenly popped out on his head. It was March, and not that hot. Fact was, there was a window open and a cool breeze was blowing in. He was sweating for a whole different reason.

"Never heard of 'em."

"That's funny," Heck said, "'cause their tracks lead right here into town."

"That may be," Cooley said. "We get strangers through here all the time, sorta like you fellas." He looked at Clint. "You a marshal, too?"

"No," Clint said, "I'm just along for the ride."

"Sorta like a one man posse?"

"That's right," Heck said, "this here's Clint Adams, my one man posse."

The sheriff's chair came forward with a thud.

"Adams?"

"That's right," Clint said.

"Look, fellas," the man said, "I'm just a small town sheriff. Whatta I know about gangs?"

"You know somethin' about this one," Heck said, "or you wouldn't be sweatin' so much."

"Me? Sweatin'?" Cooley wiped his hand across his head and it came away soaking wet. "Hell, I sweat when somebody lights a match. Don't mean nothin'."

"You sweat when you're afraid, Sheriff," Clint said. "What are you afraid of?"

"Well," Sheriff Cooley said, "for one thing . . . you."

"Then tell us what we want to know and we'll be on our way," Clint said.

Heck leaned his palms on the man's desk and loomed over him.

"Come on, Sheriff. Whatever they told you they want you to tell us. They're leavin' us a trail a mile wide as it is."

"Well . . . I ain't sure, mind you."

"Tell us, anyway."

"I think they mighta left some boys waitin' for you at the other end of town . . . fer when you ride out."

"And would those boys know where the gang is headed?"

"All them boys know is the few bucks they got paid."

"To kill us?"

"I dunno—"

"More than likely to slow us down," Clint said.

"Keep us hungry, is more like it," Heck said. "Frank knows every time he has somebody shoot at me I just get madder."

"Look," Cooley said, "the gang rode in and they rode out. Didn't even stay overnight." Then something occurred to him. "Uh, you fellas ain't stayin' overnight, are ya?"

"Not stayin' any longer than we have to, Sheriff," Heck said. "See, we don't like this place much."

"Tell you the truth," Cooley said, "me, neither. Only I ain't got much of a choice."

"I hate lawmen like that," Heck said, when they'd stepped back outside.

"Ah, he hates himself, too, Heck," Clint said. "Forget about him. What do you want to do about these jaspers waiting for us at the edge of town?"

Heck sighed and said, "Hell, we might as well go and give them their money's worth."

THIRTEEN

"When are they coming?" Russ Newton asked.

"They'll be along directly," Neal Doyle said. "They ain't got no reason to stay in town."

"What about a beer?" Newton asked.

"Naw, Mr. Sunday said they wouldn't stop for no beer," Doyle said. "He said they'd be leavin' right away."

Newton looked over at Matt Hunt. "You sure you saw them ride into town?"

"Clear as day," Hunt said. "Mr. Sunday described the marshal to a fair-thee-well."

"And the other feller?" Newton asked. "Did you see him?"

"Well, sure," Hunt said. "He was ridin' in right next ta Marshal Thomas."

"Well, who was he?"

"I dunno who he was," Hunt said. "I just seen him."

"If they don't come along soon . . ."

Both Hunt and Newton looked at Doyle, and when he didn't continue Newton said, "What?"

Doyle stared at him.

"Never mind."

53

All three men had their backs pressed to the wall of an abandoned building on the end of town.

"Matt, stick your head out and see if they're comin'," Russ Newton said.

Hunt started to obey, but then looked back and asked, "Why do I have ta be the one ta stick my head out?"

"Because you're standin' by the end of the buildin', ain't ya," Newton said.

Hunt thought about that, then said, "Oh, okay."

He stuck his head out, took a quick look, and then ducked back.

"I don't see nobody."

"Russ, you sure we can do this?" Doyle asked.

"Neal, you heard what Mr. Sunday said," Newton told him. "If we do this we can join his gang and get out of here."

"I know," Doyle said. "I heard him."

"You wanna get out of Vega, don't ya?" Newton asked.

"Yeah."

"And you wanna join Mr. Sunday's gang?"

"I guess."

"Then what's the problem?"

Doyle shrugged and said, "I guess I'm just not sure about . . . ya know, the killin' part."

"Yeah," Matt Hunt said. He looked down at the pistol that was stuck into his belt. "I guess I ain't so sure about that part, either."

Newton was standing between the other two, so he had to move his head from side to side to look at both of them.

"Yer tellin' me this now?"

Hunt sort of shrugged and Doyle just looked down at his boots.

"We got guns," Newton said. "They're loaded."

Doyle looked down at the gun he held in his hand, an old Navy Colt, and said, "I don't even know if this'll shoot."

Hunt took a peek at the gun and said, "Looks to me like it'll blow up in your hand."

"Yeah, I thought of that."

"Why didn't you bring a better gun?" Newton asked.

"This was all I could find!" Doyle complained.

"You two are useless!" Newton complained. "I'm gonna have ta do this myself."

From behind them a voice said, "I don't think you're gonna have to do it at all."

They all turned and saw Marshal Heck Thomas standing there, his hand on his gun. At that moment Clint stepped around from the corner to take a look.

"Jesus, Heck," he said, "these are just kids."

"I ain't no kid," Russ Newton said. "I'm sixteen."

FOURTEEN

The three boys sat in the sheriff's office, looking down at the floor. Russ Newton was sixteen, as he said, but the other two boys were only fourteen.

When they marched the three boys into the lawman's office Heck demanded, "Did you know the fellas waitin' for us at the end of town was kids?"

"Well . . ."

"Get out!" Heck said.

"Wha—this is my office."

Clint went around the desk, grabbed the sheriff's arm and helped him to his feet.

"You heard the marshal," he said. "Out."

"I need my gun—"

"You don't need your gun."

"What about my hat?"

Clint grabbed the man's hat, jammed it onto his head and walked him out the door.

"Hey," Matt Hunt said, "he's the sheriff. Can you do that?"

"Shut up!" Heck Thomas said.

That's when all three boys decided to look down at the floor.

"Your name's Russ?" he asked Newton.

"Yes, sir."

"You're the oldest, right?"

"Yes, sir."

"Why would you get these other two involved in somethin' like this?" Heck asked. "Did you really intend to kill us? Two men you never even saw before?"

"Mr. Sunday said we could be in his gang if we did it."

"Mr. Sunday figured we'd probably kill you," Heck said. "Do you know who I am?"

"No, sir," Newton said. "He just said you was a marshal."

"Marshal Heck Thomas, from Judge Parker's court," Heck said. "You ever heard of me?"

Newton stared at Heck and said, "Yes, sir."

"This here is Clint Adams," Heck said. "You know who he is?"

"The Gunsmith?" Doyle asked, his eyes popping wide.

"That's right," Heck said.

"Jesus, Russ," Hunt said. "You sent us against the Gunsmith?"

"I didn't know!" Newton complained.

Clint walked over to the desk where the boys' three guns were.

"Where'd you get these guns?" he asked.

"Mine's my pa's," Doyle said.

"He doesn't take very good care of it."

"It's an old one."

"Son," Clint said, "this weapon would have exploded and taken off your hand."

"I tol' you!" Hunt said.

"These other two aren't much better," Clint said.

"You boys got parents?" Heck asked.

"Yes, sir," Newton said. "I live with my ma."

"I live with my pa," Doyle said.

Heck looked at Matt Hunt, who didn't look the fourteen he claimed to be.

"I live with my ma and pa."

"You ain't gonna tell 'em, are ya?" Doyle asked.

Heck looked at Clint. If they took the time to walk these kids home and explain to their parents what they'd done they wouldn't get out of town until after dark. They couldn't afford that. Heck figured he'd already lost enough time waiting for Clint to arrive in Amarillo.

"I tell you what," Heck said. "You boys answer all my questions and we won't go to your parents."

None of the three boys spoke.

"Well?" Heck asked.

"Okay," Newton, the spokesman, said.

"Can we get our guns back?" Hunt asked.

"No," Clint said.

"How we gonna explain that to our parents?" Doyle demanded.

"That's your problem," Clint said. "Now just shut up and answer the marshal when he talks to you."

As it turned out the boys knew nothing. Sunday had come to town, picked the boys up off the street and made them his offer after telling them who he was.

"Did you ever hear of him before?" Heck asked.

"No," Newton said, "but he had a whole gang with him."

"How many men?"

"Six."

They knew that, already.

In the end they just let the boys go.

"Next time you might not be so lucky," Heck told them. "Somebody else woulda just killed you."

"Don't worry, Marshal," Doyle said. "We learned our lesson."

"Russ?" Heck said. "You're the oldest. You learn your lesson?"

"Yes, sir," he said, glumly.

"Now get out."

All three boys stood up and headed for the door. Matt Hunt, the smallest—Clint figured he was really about twelve—turned and said to Clint, "Mister, are you really the Gunsmith?"

"Yes," Clint said, "I'm really the Gunsmith."

For a moment the boy looked like he was going to faint, and then he hurriedly followed his friends out the door.

FIFTEEN

Clint and Heck left Vega, traveled for a few more hours, and then made camp in a clearing near a creek.

"We probably should've talked to those kids' parents," Clint said when they were eating.

"We couldn't afford the time," Heck said. "I think meeting you and finding out they almost threw down on you pretty much scared them."

"I hope so."

They had a simple meal of beans and coffee, and when they were done Clint made a second pot.

"I wonder what kind of sick satisfaction Frank Sunday got from sending those kids to be killed?"

"It's just the killing," Heck said. "He likes it, and if he ain't doin' it himself he likes settin' somebody else up to do it."

"Well, I don't appreciate being set up to kill a bunch of kids," Clint said.

"He made you mad."

"Yeah."

"Good."

They had discussed setting watches when they left Amarillo. It was true that they were the trackers and that

61

nobody was tracking them, but it was clear they never knew when somebody was going to come after them. The safest thing to do was stand watch.

"I'll take the first watch," Clint said. "I'll wake you in four hours."

"Fine," Heck said, rolling himself up in his bedroll. "Since you can't possibly find a girl out here in the middle of nowhere maybe I'll actually get some sleep, this time."

"You're a sad and lonely man, Heck Thomas."

"Yeah," Heck said, "tell that to my wife."

Heck rolled over and in moments he was snoring. Clint poured himself yet another cup of coffee and settled down on a rock. He made a point of not looking into the fire, as he didn't want to have to wait for his night vision to return.

He recalled the looks on the faces of the three boys when they had left the sheriff's office. It was his fervent hope that they were scared enough to forget about joining up with an outlaw gang and about ever killing someone. It wasn't bad enough that Frank Sunday was a madman and a murderer, he had to try to corrupt young boys and turn them into killers, as well—or worse, get them killed.

There was no two ways about it. Any man who could do that to a bunch of kids had to be stopped.

Clint woke the next morning with Heck Thomas's big boot prodding him.

"I'm awake," he complained.

"Come on, I got coffee ready, and some beans."

"Beans for breakfast?"

"Easiest thing to carry," Heck said, "especially when you want to travel light. You know that as well as I do."

Clint was used to traveling light. He'd ridden in many posses, but they were usually made up of town merchants and didn't last more than a day or two. He'd also ridden the trail tracking outlaws with Wyatt Earp and Bat Masterson and even Heck Thomas, before. He knew you couldn't track dragging a packhorse with you every foot of the way. Not if you wanted to ever catch up to whoever you were tracking.

Clint got to his feet and stumbled towards the fire. Heck handed him a cup of coffee and a plate of beans. They sat down across from each other and began to eat.

"You got to stop thinkin' about those boys," Heck said.

"Huh?"

"I can see it in your face."

"Sorry," Clint said. "But thinking about them is just going to keep me mad at Frank Sunday."

"Believe me," Heck said, "you're gonna find plenty of other reasons before we catch up with him."

A few miles outside of Tucumcari, New Mexico, seven men rode up upon a ranch house. Inside the house Horace Turnbull, his wife Eunice, and their fourteen-year-old daughter, Julie, were finishing up the breakfast dishes. Well, the two women were. Horace was finishing up an extra cup of coffee he'd chosen to have, which was the reason he was still there instead of out rounding up strays with his two hands, Buddy and Brad.

"Pa," Julie said, "riders."

She could see them from the kitchen window.

"How many?"

"Seven."

Horace stood up and took his Springfield down from its pegs on the wall.

"I'll see what they want."

"Horace," Eunice said, "you be careful."

"Just stay inside," he warned them. "Both of you."

He stepped out onto the porch and pulled shut the door of the four room cabin he'd built with his bare hands. By this time the seven men had reached the house and stopped, fanned out single file.

"Can I help you gents?" he asked. He was not holding the rifle in a threatening manner, just cradling it.

"You sure can," Frank Sunday said. He drew his gun before Horace could react and shot the rancher through the forehead.

SIXTEEN

Days later Clint and Heck came upon two dead men. They dismounted to examine the bodies.

"Shot from a distance," Heck said. "In the back."

"Mine, too."

They stood up and looked around, but there was nothing for them to see.

"What's the nearest town?" Clint asked.

"Tucumcari, I think."

"Maybe they work at a nearby ranch."

"Let's ride," Heck said. "If we come to a ranch we'll ask. If we come to a town we'll send someone back for them."

"Some scavengers have been at them already," Clint said. "I bet they've been lying here four or five days. If we leave them any longer—"

"Clint," Heck said, "they're dead, they've been violated already. There's nothing we can do."

"We can bury the poor bastards."

"What if they got family waitin' for them?" Heck asked. "Best to leave them and find somebody we can tell."

Clint was still hesitant, but in the end he gave in. They mounted up and kept riding.

• • •

It was almost an hour later when they came within sight of
a house. It was small, with a barn and corral next to it.
There were no horses in the corral, and the gate was wide
open.

"I don't like this," Heck said.

"There's something on the porch."

They rode closer, until the body on the porch became
clear.

"Damn," Clint said.

They rode up to the house with their hands on their
guns, but it was clear there was no longer any danger, and
nothing they could do. They dismounted.

"Shot through the head," Clint said. "One shot."

"Rifle over here," Heck said. He picked up the Springfield. "Wasn't fired."

"I guess we better check inside," Clint said.

As bad as it had been to find the bodies of the two men,
and then the third man on the porch, what greeted them inside was infinitely worse.

Two bodies, both wearing dresses. They split up to
check one each.

"Fella outside must have been the pa," Heck said. "This
here looks like the ma, and it looks like she mighta put up
a fight."

"She was probably trying to protect this one," Clint
said. "Daughter, looks thirteen or fourteen."

The girl's dress was up around her waist, and there was
blood between her legs. Clint lowered the dress and turned
away.

"They raped her," he said. "Then looks like they strangled her. Don't know if they were done or not when she
was killed."

"Wouldn't matter to these animals if she was alive or
dead," Heck said. "I told you they were bad."

"What about her?"

Heck looked down at the mother. He was about to raise her dress when he saw that some blood had seeped through.

"Yeah, they raped her, too," Heck said. "Probably started when she was alive."

"How was she killed?"

Heck frowned, looked down at her again. Other than the blood seeping through the dress from between her legs there weren't any marks on her.

"I think she just . . . died while they were having her."

"Maybe her heart just stopped."

"Maybe it was the horror," Heck said. "Bein' raped, hearin' her daughter scream while they raped her, too. Knowin' that her man was dead."

"I hear you, Heck," Clint said. "I know what happened. So what do you want to do now?"

"What do you mean?"

"You want to leave these people here too?" Clint asked. "Not bury 'em?"

"Might be better if we see if there's a wagon in the barn," Heck said. "We can hitch it up and take them into Tucumcari. They can have a proper burial there."

"What about the other two out there?"

"We can go and pick them up, too."

Clint looked around the house. It had been ransacked, but it was a pretty safe bet that these people didn't have much of value. There might have been some horses in the corral outside . . .

"We'll need horses to hitch up a wagon," he said.

"We'll look for some," Heck said. "Even if Sunday and his men got fresh horses here theirs should still be out there, somewhere."

"Okay," Clint said, taking a deep breath, "okay."

They walked outside, looked down at the dead man again.

"You were right," Clint said.

"About what?"

"You said I'd have more reason to hate Frank Sunday before we caught up to them," Clint said. "You were right."

SEVENTEEN

It caused quite a stir when Heck Thomas and Clint Adams rode into Tucumcari with a wagonload of bodies. They had tried to cover the corpses with some blankets from the house, but during the trip they had slid off and as they rode down the main street of town there were some arms and legs visible. By the time they got to the sheriff's office the man was waiting outside for them. The sun glinted brightly off his badge, which meant he kept it well-shined. Clint hope he wasn't the kind of man who took better care of his tin than he did his town.

"Word spreads fast," Heck said to the lawman as he dismounted. Clint was driving the wagon, with Eclipse tied to the back of it.

"Bad news travels fast," the sheriff said. "Who are you, and who do you have back there?"

"My name's Heck Thomas," Heck said, "Deputy Marshal out of Judge Parker's court."

"That's the Territories," the sheriff said. "What are you doin' this far West?"

"Chasing the Frank Sunday gang," Heck said. "We think they did this. As to who this is, we don't have any idea. We sorta hoped you'd know."

"You a marshal, too?" the sheriff asked Clint.

"My name's Clint Adams. I'm a volunteer."

The lawman studied both men for a few moments. It was clear he'd heard of both of them. He was in his forties, and they couldn't tell how long he'd been working as a lawman. The shiny badge could have meant he was new, but it also could have meant he had a lot of time on his hands in a quiet town.

"My name's Ed Wright," he said, finally. "Been the law here for over twelve years. I should be able to tell you who they are, but I got a bad feelin' I already know. You got a little girl back there? Fourteen or so?"

"I'm afraid so."

"Damn," Wright said. "That's Horace Turnbull and his family. We wondered why we ain't seen them for a while."

"Anybody think to go out and check on them?" Clint wondered aloud.

The sheriff took offense.

"We pretty much mind our own business around here, Mr. Adams. Horace and his family would come into town once a week, maybe every two weeks, for supplies. We ain't seen 'em for three, but that don't mean we're gonna go ridin' out there to check on them."

Wright stepped into the street and lifted the blankets from the faces of the dead.

"Jesus," he said. "You got Bud Carter and his brother Brad back here, too. They worked for Horace."

"They were shot in the back," Clint said.

"Horace is drilled through the head," Wright said, looking at the rancher's face. "The women?"

"Raped," Heck said. "Killed. Looks like the mother's heart just gave out. Little girl was strangled."

Wright dropped the blanket back over the faces as townspeople moved in for a closer look. Before long Clint realized he and the wagon were surrounded by people who weren't looking too happy.

"How do we know they didn't kill Horace and his family?" somebody shouted.

Wright looked at Heck, who pulled aside his jacket to show his badge.

"Wearin' a badge don't mean he didn't kill 'em," somebody else yelled.

"Yeah, the other one ain't wearin' a badge!"

Clint shifted in his seat, giving him easier access to his gun just in case things turned uglier.

"Be sensible," Heck said. He was speaking to the lawman but loud enough for all to hear. "If we'd killed 'em why would we bring 'em in? We woulda skirted your town and just kept goin'."

"Good point," Wright admitted. He turned to address the townspeople. "Okay, folks, I'm gonna need you to go about your business. I'll need some volunteers to take the bodies to the undertaker. Ned, Al, you boys just volunteered."

Two young men in their twenties stepped forward as the rest of the crowd reluctantly dispersed.

"Adams, you can step down. These boys'll take care of the bodies. You and the marshal can come inside and tell me about this Frank Sunday gang."

Clint dropped to the ground, relieved that he hadn't had to draw his gun against the crowd. He untied Eclipse's reins from the back of the wagon—actually, a buckboard—and tied the animal next to Heck Thomas's horse at the hitching rail in front of the sheriff's office. As he mounted the boardwalk to follow Wright and Heck into the office he noticed a few men were still milling about, giving him hard looks.

"Were Turnbull and his family well-liked, Sheriff?" he asked as he closed the door behind them.

"Not particularly," Wright said, seating himself at his desk. "Folks just don't take kindly to strangers ridin' into town with dead bodies."

The office was small, typical of most western sheriffs'

offices, with a desk, a stove, a gun rack, some extra chairs, and a cell block in the back.

"Have a seat, gents," Wright invited. He opened the bottom drawer of his desk and pulled out a bottle of rye. "Looks to me like you can use a drink."

"I could probably use two after the morning we've had," Heck said and Clint, more of a beer drinker than a whiskey drinker, had to agree.

EIGHTEEN

As Clint Adams went into the sheriff's office four men who hadn't quite dispersed with the rest of the town crossed the street and took up positions in front of the hardware store.

"Whataya think?" Tom Bass asked.

"I think I didn't really like ol' Horace that much, but that little gal of his sure was pretty," Zack Wyler said. "A few more years she woulda been worth askin' to a dance, or somethin'."

"More like takin' into a barn," Bill Trent said with a grin, "or somethin'."

"Hey!" Wyler said. "Have some respect for the dead, damn it."

"So, what are we gonna do?" the fourth man, Dave McNab, asked. While the others were in their mid-twenties, McNab was the youngest, at eighteen. He, too, thought that Julie Grant had been pretty. In fact, he'd been thinking about courting her. Now she was gone. "We can't just sit here. We gotta do somethin'."

"Like what?" Wyler asked.

"Well . . . somebody's gotta pay!"

"We still don't know that them two didn't do it," Trent said.

73

None of the four of them had heard the names of the two men who were in with the sheriff. If they had they might not have been thinking about making trouble. As it was they were on the prod, looking for a fight, or a reason to.

"Let's wait and see where they go when they come out," Wyler said.

"And then we'll take 'em?" Dave asked.

"And then we'll go have a drink or two, Dave," Wyler said, "and decide."

Sheriff Wright had two shot glasses and a coffee mug for the whiskey. Clint and Heck accepted the glasses while the sheriff poured himself a healthy mug full of rye. The man settled back with his mug and listened to Heck's story.

"Sounds like they're just continuing what they started in the Territories," he commented when Heck was done.

"They don't know no other way," Heck said.

"You make 'em sound like animals with no will of their own," Wright said.

"Oh, they got will of their own," Heck said. "I ain't makin' excuses for 'em. They're all killers. They deserve to be put down."

"Is that what you're gonna do?" Wright asked. "You and Mr. Adams, here? Put 'em down?"

"We're gonna bring 'em back to the judge's court, if we can," Heck said. "If we can't . . ."

"The decision will be theirs, Sheriff," Clint added.

"Well," Wright said, "you two against . . . what, seven of them? With your reps and all? I guess that's about fair."

"Unless you want to come along," Heck said. "Throw in with us."

"Yeah," Clint said, "having you along would give us more official standing."

Neither of them expected the man to agree, but they enjoyed the panicked look on his face as he tried to think of a way out.

"You boys expect to catch up with them in New Mexico?"

"Don't rightly know, Sheriff," Heck said.

"Well," Wright said, "I really can't leave town. I got responsibilities here."

"You could put together a posse," Heck said. "After all, they did kill five people in your jurisdiction."

"Well," Wright said, thinking fast, "technically they was killed outside of town. I mean, I'm the town lawman, not a county lawman. I'm paid by the town, so I can't rightly just go traipsing off. Besides, with you two on their trail they'll pay sooner or later, right?"

"You got that right, Sheriff," Heck said, standing up. "They will pay sooner or later."

Clint stood and he and Heck put their glasses on the man's desk.

"Obliged for the drink, Sheriff," Heck said.

"You boys gonna be stayin' in town overnight?"

"Don't figure we got a choice," Heck said. "The horses have to be at least as tired as us."

"We'll be starting out at first light, though," Clint said. "I hope your people can control themselves between now and then."

"This ain't a town of troublemakers, Adams," Wright said.

"Sheriff," Heck said, "every town's got troublemakers. They just need a good reason, or the right amount of liquor in 'em."

"How many hotels you got?" Clint asked.

"Two," the sheriff said. "You should be able to get a room in either one of them."

"What about a meal?" Clint asked. "Maybe a good steak?"

"Down the street, Denny's Café. Denny, he's the cook and the owner. Tell him I sent you down."

"We'll do that."

"Well," Heck said, "again, obliged for the drink."

Wright decided to stand, but remained behind his desk.

"Thanks for bringin' them in," he said, shaking hands with both men. "We'll see they get buried good and proper."

Clint and Heck nodded and went out the door. Across the street three or four men were standing, or leaning, apparently waiting for the two of them to come out. They were all wearing guns.

"Some of those troublemakers you were talking about," Clint commented.

"Yeah," Heck said. "Not enough liquor in them, though."

"Not yet, anyway."

NINETEEN

Clint and Heck both found the steaks at Denny's Café to their liking. Heck was a bit put out that the waitress apparently found Clint to her liking, to the point of giving him extra vegetables on his plate and—according to him, although Clint didn't see it—a larger steak.

"I'm as hungry as you are," he grumbled.

"Yeah, but you're also married."

"How does she know that?"

"Come on, Heck," Clint said. "Women can tell."

"I look married?"

"Look it," Clint said, "sound it, act it."

Heck thought that over for a few moments and then said, "That's still no reason to give you extra food."

Denny Boyd, the owner, came out then, to check and see how they liked their food. He was giving them extra attention because they had dropped the sheriff's name, and because he knew they had brought in Horace Turnbull, his family, and the Carter brothers.

Clint held his breath while Heck answered, but all his friend said was, "It was a fine meal, Mr. Boyd. We thank you."

"How about some more coffee? And two hunks of my apple pie? Denny asked.

"Sounds good," Clint said.

"I'll have Angie bring it right over."

"Watch," Heck said, as Denny walked away, "she's gonna bring you a bigger piece."

"If she does," Clint said, "I'll trade with you."

"Ah," Heck said, with a wave of his hand. "It don't matter. I'm not really upset about that, it's . . ."

"Sunday."

"The sonofabitch has to be stopped, Clint!" Heck said, in a rush. "I just wish we could figure out where he's going and get there first."

"Maybe we should try doing that."

"Try thinking like a crazy man?" Heck asked.

"Why not?" Clint asked. "We can get hold of a map tomorrow and see what happens."

Heck rubbed his face hard with both hands.

"I guess we could try it," he said, finally. "Makes more sense to follow the trail, but . . . what the hell."

At that point Angie came over with two pieces of pie and set them down in front of the two men. Clint waited for the explosion, but Heck simply said to her, "Thank you."

"I'll bring more coffee."

"Thanks, Angie," Clint said.

As she left Heck said, "That must be your trick."

"What trick?" Clint asked.,

"Callin' them by their names," Heck said. "You call waitresses by their names. That's why they like you."

"Well," Clint said, "they have names for a reason."

Heck took a bite of his pie and said, "It's real good."

"And," Clint said, "they're the same size."

Heck nodded, was about to say something when the girl returned with the coffee pot. She filled both cups, gave Clint a smile and went back to the kitchen.

"What?" Clint asked.

Heck looked at him.

"You were going to say something before she came over."

"Oh, nothin'," Heck said. He sipped his coffee and put it down. "Everything's fine. Coffee's good, pie's good . . ."

"Heck."

"What?"

"We'll catch up to him," Clint said. "Him and his whole gang."

"I just don't know—" Heck started, then stopped. Then he started again. "I just don't know how they could do that to a young girl. I mean, what's the point?"

"When you're loco," Clint said, "there doesn't have to be a point."

"What was the point of doin' that to her?" Dave McNab asked. "I jus' don't get it."

"Ain't no point to somethin' like that," Tom Bass said. He poured some more whiskey into a glass for the kid.

"Stop givin' him so much," Zach Wyler complained.

"Afraid he's gonna get drunk?" Bill Trent asked.

"No," Wyler said, "I'm afraid there won't be enough for the rest of us."

"It was them," McNab said.

"Who?" Wyler asked.

"Them two," McNab said. "That marshal and his pal. I bet he ain't even a real marshal."

"Prolly not," Bass agreed. Of the four the kid was the most drunk, but Bass wasn't far behind.

"We oughtta do somethin' about it," McNab said. "We should make them pay."

"The whole town's talkin' about it," Trent said to Wyler. "Maybe the kid's got a point."

"Horace Turnbull wasn't my best friend," Wyler said.

"Hell," Bass said, "ol' Horace weren't anybody's best friend, but he was from around here."

"Yeah," McNab said, "we gotta protect our own."

"Avenge," Wyler said.

"What?" Trent asked.

Wyler looked around the table at his comrades.

"We gotta avenge our own," he said. "We can't protect 'em. They're already dead. We gotta get revenge for 'em."

"We ain't the law," Trent said.

"The law ain't gonna do nothin'," Wyler said. "Sheriff Wright's been the law for too long around here. He's gotten fat and lazy. Now, we gotta do it ourselves. We gotta show people they can't come around here and just kill people."

"How do we do that?" Bill Trent asked.

"We have some more drinks all around," Wyler said, picking up the bottle.

They all held their glasses out to be filled.

"Then what?" McNab asked, his eyes shining with heat.

"Drink up," Wyler said. "Since you're so damned put out about what they did to that gal, Dave, you're gonna have a big part in this plan."

"And what plan is that, Zack?" Bill Trent asked

"I don't care what the plan is," McNab said. He downed the drink and slammed the shot glass down on the table. "I'll do it!"

TWENTY

When Clint and Heck Thomas left the café Heck said, "I need a cold beer."

"Think that's a good idea?" Clint asked. "We got clean sheets waiting for us."

They had each gotten a room in Tucumcari's largest hotel—which wasn't saying much.

"Fresh sheets," Clint said, "and a real mattress. We been on the trail a while, Heck. Let's get a good night's sleep."

"One beer," Heck said.

Clint sighed.

"The sheriff wants us to stay out of trouble."

"How much trouble can one beer make?" Heck asked.

Clint thought he knew the answer to that, but in the end he agreed and they went in search of a saloon.

When Clint Adams and Heck Thomas entered Big Al's Saloon they were spotted immediately by Dave McNab.

"They're here!" he hissed to his friends.

Trent and Wyler had to turn to look, while Bass only had to move his head slightly.

"They got a nerve," Bass said.

"What do we do, Zack?" McNab asked, anxiously. "What do we do?"

"Just relax," Wyler said. "We got time."

McNab followed them with his eyes as they walked to the bar and beckoned to the bartender.

"They done it," he said. "I know they done it."

"Even if they didn't," the drunken Bass said, "somebody's gotta pay, right?"

"Right," Wyler said. "We got to make an example of somebody so it don't happen again."

"Now?" McNab asked. "Now, Zack?"

"Let 'em have their beer, Dave," Wyler said. "Man deserves a last beer before he dies."

"They don't," McNab said, with feeling. "They don't deserve nothin' after what they done."

"Relax, Dave," Zack Wyler said. "All of you just relax and wait until I call it."

"You see what I see?" Heck asked as soon as they entered the saloon.

"I see 'em," Clint said.

"Looks like they're gettin' liquored up."

"Heck," Clint said, "you weren't looking for them, were you?"

"Why would I be lookin' for them?" Heck asked. "All I want is a beer, Clint. Come on."

Clint followed Heck to the bar, where the marshal waved at the bartender.

"Two beers."

The bartender came over and glared at them.

"Whataya fellas want here?" he demanded.

"Just what I said," Heck answered. "Two beers."

"We don't serve your kind here."

The bartender was middle-aged with a receding hairline and an expanding waist line.

"What kind is that?" Heck asked. "The kind that's

gonna drag your sorry ass across the bar and slap the ship out of you if you don't give us two beers? That kind?"

The bartender blinked, backed away a few feet, then said, "Uh, okay, two beers, comin' up."

As he went to draw two mugs Clint said, "I told you we should've gone to the hotel."

"A quick beer, Clint, and then we're gone."

The saloon was doing a brisk business that evening, and Clint could feel that most of the eyes in the place were on them. There were no gaming tables in the place, but there were a couple of poker games going on, and the players were about the only ones not watching them. A couple of saloon girls were making the rounds of the floor, shooting glances over at them every so often, and staying away from them.

The bartender came over and set two beers on the bar, then moved away quickly.

"Guess we shoulda just left those bodies out there," Heck said, "or buried them in the spot, like you wanted to. Don't look like this town takes too kindly to us bringin' them in for a decent burial."

"They're just scared," Clint said. "In shock."

"Ain't like they never seen death before," Heck said. "It's all around them."

Clint picked up his beer and drank left-handed, leaving his right hand free. He drank half the beer down and set the mug back on the bar. He had to admit it went down pretty good after their meal. He noticed Heck had only taken a couple of sips of his.

"Come on, Heck," he said. "Drink up and let's get out of here. This place is a powder keg and somebody's bound to light the fuse."

"Come on, Zack!" Dave McNab pleaded. "Lemme do it. I can handle a gun. You seen me."

"Yeah, I seen you."

Fact was, of the four of them the kid handled a gun the best. He was fast and he was accurate. But he was young, and stupid. Wyler looked over at the two old-timers at the bar. Maybe the kid could handle one of them, but not two. No, the rest of them would have to back him up.

"So which one you want, kid?" he asked.

"The badge," McNab said, right away. "I want the one claims he's a marshal."

"Boys," he said, "I'll back Dave's play. The other one belongs to you."

"Uh, wait a minute," Bill Trent said. He was the least liquored up of the four.

"What is it, Bill?"

"Are we gonna kill 'em?"

"What'd you think we was gonna do?" Dave McNab asked. "Kiss 'em?"

"Shut up, Dave," Trent said. "Zack? We killin' these two men?"

"You saw what they did to Horace and his family, Bill," Wyler said. "What would you have us do?"

"We ain't sure they done it," Trent said. "The sheriff didn't arrest them."

"I told you," Wyler said, "the sheriff ain't no good. This is up to us."

"Come on, Zack," Trent said. "That's the liquor talkin'."

"Kid?" Wyler said to McNab. "You up for this?"

"I'm up for it, Zack!" the kid said, enthusiastically.

Wyler looked across the table at Trent.

"You gonna let this kid show you up, Bill?" he asked. "He's ready. Why ain't you?"

"'Cause he ain't got the stomach for it," McNab said. "He ain't got the guts."

"I told you to shut up, Dave," Trent said.

"Come on, Bill," Tom Bass said. "You ain't gonna let a wet-behind-the-ears kid show you up, are ya?"

Trent looked over at Bass and saw in his eyes the same

thing he saw in Wyler's and McNab's. They'd all been drinking faster than him, and they were all hopped up on the kind of guts you got from liquor—the kind that got you killed.

But they were his friends, and if they were going to do this he couldn't let them do it without him.

"All right, goddamn it," he said. "All right. If we're gonna do this then, by God, let's do it!"

TWENTY-ONE

From where he was standing Clint could see the four men having a heated conversation. It wasn't hard to guess what it was probably all about.

"Heck," he said, "we've got to go."

"I'm not finished with my beer yet," Heck said, "and neither are you. Take it easy."

"What's going on, Heck?" Clint demanded. "Are you really looking for trouble?"

Heck turned to face Clint, putting his back to the four men. Clint wondered if the two glasses of rye whiskey with the sheriff were still in Heck's system. It didn't seem so during dinner, but now his eyes seemed to be blazing. Maybe the beer had started the fire in his belly, again.

"I just want to do somethin', Clint," Heck said. "After what I've seen over the past few months . . . somebody needs to pay."

"So you just want to shoot somebody?" Clint asked. "Anybody? Is that it?"

"I don't know," the lawman said morosely. "Maybe."

"Well, those four men behind you feel the same way," Clint said. "They're liquored up now, got their courage up, and they just want to shoot somebody. You want to oblige them? Kill a couple of them?"

Heck turned and looked at the table of four friends. The young one was getting to his feet, and the others were following, although one seemed reluctant.

"I guess you're right," Heck said. "We better get out of here."

"Now you're talking."

Clint took Heck's arm and they turned for the door, but it was too late.

"Hold on there, gents!" Dave McNab called. "You ain't goin' anywhere."

As soon as the words were out of his mouth Bill Trent knew there was no turning back. He didn't know why Zack Wyler had given the kid his head, but he had, and now they were all getting dragged along.

Trent hoped that the kid was as good with a gun as they all thought he was.

Zach Wyler fell in behind Dave McNab, with Trent fanned to one side and Tom Bass to the other. The other three didn't know it, but they were going to shield him and allow him to make his move. McNab may have been faster with a gun, but Wyler considered himself the smart one. He was also going to be the one who came out of this standing.

"Look, son," Heck said, turning to face the boy, "we were just leavin'—"

"No," McNab said, "no, you ain't leavin' this saloon, and you ain't leavin' town. Not after what you did."

Suddenly, the rest of the patrons in the saloon realized what was going on and scattered for cover. Some tables got overturned and men tried to peer over to the top to watch the action while being out of harm's way. The bartender simply dropped down out of sight to wait out the action.

"Son, what is it you think we done?" Heck asked.

"Stop callin' me son," McNab said, "and you know what you did to Julie and her family."

"Julie—" Heck started.

"The young girl we brought in?" Clint asked. "So—what's your name?"

"Dave," the young man said, "Dave McNab."

"Dave, are you and your friends willing to slap leather over this mistake?"

"What mistake?"

"All we did was find the bodies and bring them in," Clint said. "Why do people in this town resent that?"

"I don't know what you're talkin' about!" McNab said. "I'm gonna kill you."

Clint looked past McNab to the other three. Two of them seemed as drunk as the boy, but one was looking around with wide, sober eyes, as if looking for a way out.

"You figure you got enough backup, boy?" Clint asked. "You fellas ready to die to back your friend's play?"

"Zack," Bill Trent said, "maybe he's right—"

"Shut up, Bill!" Wyler said. "Let Dave make his play."

"He's makin' his play while you hide behind him?" Heck Thomas asked.

"Whataya mean?" McNab asked.

"Your friend is standin' behind you, boy," Heck said. "He figures you'll take the first bullet. If you four are gonna stand together you better fan out more."

Now McNab's drunk eyes took on a puzzled look. He turned to look at Zack Wyler over his shoulder.

"What are you doin', Zack?"

"Just backin' your play, Dave."

"If you're backing his play," Clint said, "you should be doing it next to him, not behind him."

Zack Wyler glared at Clint over the kid's shoulder.

"Whatayou care, mister? Who are you, anyway?"

"I'm Marshal Heck Thomas," Heck said, "and this is my friend, Clint Adams."

Bill Trent reached out and grabbed Zack Wyler's shoulder.

"Clint Adams!" he repeated. "Zack, did you hear—"

"I heard," Wyler said, shrugging his friend's hand off. "He's lyin'. He ain't no Gunsmith. And this old-timer ain't no real marshal."

"I'm as real as could be," Heck said, "right outta Judge Parker's court."

"Hangin' Judge Parker?" Bill Trent asked.

"Son," Heck said to Trent, "you appear to be the sober one here, and the smart one. Talk to your friends."

"He ain't the smart one," Zack Wyler complained. "I am."

"Well," Clint said, "from here you aren't looking all that smart, friend."

"What's your name?" Heck asked Bill Trent.

"Trent . . . sir."

"Trent, if I was you I'd move on. If your friends are drunk enough to see this through that's no reason for you to get killed."

Trent looked at his three friends, but none of them looked back at him. His decision seemed easy.

"Yes, sir."

He stepped away from the other three and headed for the door.

"Bill, you coward!" Zack Wyler shouted. "Get back here."

"I ain't going against a real lawman, Zack," Trent said from the door, "and I sure as hell ain't gonna draw against the Gunsmith. You boys are on your own."

With that Bill Trent left the saloon, the batwing doors swinging behind him.

"And then there were three," Clint said, looking at the other young men.

TWENTY-TWO

"Huh?" Dave McNab said, looking completely confused.

"You boys ain't gonna go for your guns," Heck said.

"What makes you say that, old man?" Zack Wyler demanded belligerently.

"You've already talked about it too much," Clint said. "The time to draw was when you first stood up. Now the time has passed. You might as well leave."

"You gonna let him talk to you that way, Dave?" Wyler asked, prodding McNab from behind.

"He's still hidin' behind you, boy," Heck said.

"Don't call me boy!" McNab shouted. "And I don't care if he's behind me. I don't need them. I can take the two of you myself."

"You that good with a gun?" Clint asked him.

"Yeah, I'm that good."

"Prove it."

"Huh?"

"I said prove it," Clint repeated. "Show us and everybody here how good you are."

"Whataya mean?"

"Here." Clint took a step and grabbed an empty beer mug from the bar. "I'll toss this in the air and you shoot it."

91

"That's stupid!"

"Do it, Dave!" Tom Bass said, speaking for the first time. "Go ahead and do it."

"Or maybe you just ain't good enough," Heck said.

Dave McNab's body was as taut as a guitar string. Clint knew this could go one of two ways, and one way was going to end up with a dead boy—maybe more than one.

"What do you say, Dave?" Clint asked. "Do I toss it up?"

McNab moved his feet, as if getting himself more comfortable, and then said, "Okay. Go ahead."

Clint didn't wait. He tossed the beer mug into the air. It was still ascending when the boy drew and fired one shot, shattering it and sending glass around the room.

Clint couldn't believe his eyes. The boy was fast! Heck peered over his shoulder at Clint and raised his eyebrows. Suddenly, they weren't so sure they'd get out of this without gun play.

The place was dead quiet, and then suddenly some of the onlookers cheered. Tom Bass reached over and patted McNab on the back as the boy holstered his gun.

"That good enough for you?" Zack Wyler asked.

"Well," Clint said, "not quite."

"What?"

"That was a beer mug, for Chrissake," Heck said. He knew where Clint was heading. "Anybody coulda hit that."

"Did you see how fast he was?" Wyler demanded. He was truly impressed with McNab's speed.

"Speed don't always do it, boy," Clint said. "It's accuracy."

"What?" McNab asked.

"It's whether or not you can hit what you're shooting at," Clint clarified.

"I hit the damned glass!"

"How about a shot glass?" Heck asked. "Can you hit a shot glass?"

"Sure he can," Wyler said, "can't ya, Dave?"

McNab hesitated, then said, " 'Course I can."

The bartender had become interested in what was going on and stood up.

"Bartender, a shot glass," Clint said.

"Sure thing."

The man handed Clint a clean one.

"You ready?" Clint asked McNab.

"Whenever you are," the boy said, setting himself.

Clint tossed the glass up. The boy drew. He fired one shot and the glass shattered, but Clint noticed that he had caught the glass on the way down this time, not on the way up. It had taken him longer.

McNab holstered his gun as his friends pounded his back and others in the saloon cheered.

"What did you think of that?" Wyler demanded.

Clint and Heck hesitated and then Heck said, "Well, that wasn't bad."

"Wasn't bad?" Wyler demanded. "Could you do better, old man?"

"Me? No, not me," Heck said. He jerked his thumb at Clint. "Him, he can do better."

"Show us!" Wyler said.

"Yeah," McNab sneered, "if you can do better than that show us."

Heck stood up straight, looked around the room.

"Shot glass?" the bartender asked.

"No," Heck said, "too big."

He walked around the room, as if he was seeking something specific. Finally, he plucked something from a table and returned to the bar.

"This," he said.

He held a red poker chip in his hand. He looked at Clint, who nodded. It would be harder than the glasses not only because it was smaller, but it was lighter. Any kind of breeze could throw the shot off.

"Ready?" he asked Clint.

"Ready."

Heck didn't toss the chip into the air, but flipped it so that it spun. Clint drew and fired, and right in the middle of a spin he drilled the red chip dead center. It fell to the floor. Heck picked it up and held it for all to see.

There was a stunned silence.

TWENTY-THREE

"Dave can do that!" Zack Wyler said, confidently.

Clint could tell from the look in Dave McNab's eyes that he wasn't as sure as his friend was.

"Uh, sure I can."

"Okay," Heck said. "I'll toss another chip in the air. If your friend misses, you boys leave the saloon."

"And if he hits it," Wyler said, "you gotta throw down with him."

"I do?" Heck asked.

"No," Wyler said, pointing at Clint, "he does."

Heck didn't even both to look over at Clint for confirmation.

"Done!"

He went to a poker table and grabbed a chip, this time a white one. He returned to the bar and looked at Dave McNab.

"You ready, boy?"

"I'm ready."

Again, Heck flipped the chip rather than toss it in the air. The boy drew and fired, and the chip fell to the floor. Heck retrieved it quickly and held it up for all to see.

"A miss."

McNab jammed his gun back into his holster.

"Damn! I coulda swore I hit it!"

"That don't mean nothin'," Wyler complained.

"It means you and your boys are leavin'," Heck said. "Bye, bye."

Clint thought it probably would have worked if Heck hadn't tossed in those last words.

"Who you think you're talkin' to, old man?" McNab asked.

"I'll tell you who I'm talkin' to," Heck said, facing the boy square. "A little pissant who talks too much. You wanna do this, boy? Okay, let's do it. You don't even have to draw down on Clint Adams. I'll take you myself."

"Heck—" Clint said.

"No, no," Heck said, "the boy's got this comin', Clint. You handle the other two?"

"Well, sure."

"You two boys ready to draw on the Gunsmith?" Heck asked. "You, with the big mouth. You gonna step out from behind yer friend, now?"

"Zack—" Tom Bass said. His eyes had widened at the speed with which Clint had shot the red chip, and seeing McNab miss the white one he now wasn't sure he wanted to be involved.

"Sure," Wyler said, "sure, I'll step out from behind him."

"But he didn't. Instead he pushed McNab as hard as he could into Heck Thomas and went for his gun. Clint killed him before he could clear leather. Tom Bass, seeing what was happening, panicked and tried to get his gun out. Since McNab's speed with a gun had come as a total surprise to him Clint couldn't take a chance with the others. He shot Tom Bass dead before he realized how dead slow the man was.

Heck had held onto McNab as long as he could. The boy fought him like a wild cat. Finally, Heck pushed him away from him. The boy turned and moved his hand to-wards his gun.

"Go ahead, boy!" Heck said, standing ready. "Your friends are dead, you might as well join 'em."

Heck caught the boy's eyes and held them.

"Ever killed a man before, son?" he asked. "Ever looked into a man's eyes just before you kill him? Just before he dies? Come on, boy, you're still hesitatin'. Draw or go home."

McNab took a moment to look down at his fallen comrades. He stared at them with a mixture of pain and puzzlement, then moved his hand away from his gun, walked past Clint and Heck out onto the street.

Heck turned and put his elbows on the bar, right next to the white poker chip.

"Guess it was a good thing the boy missed, huh?" Clint asked.

Heck took another white chip from his pocket and laid it on the bar next to the first one. This one had a neat hole drilled through it.

"Who says he missed?"

TWENTY-FOUR

"I asked you both nicely to stay out of trouble," Sheriff Ed Wright said.

They were back in his office, sitting in front of him like two schoolboys being scolded.

"We tried to avoid it, Sheriff," Clint said.

"I know that," Wright said. "Everybody in the saloon says you gave those boys every chance to walk out. Luckily, two of them did, or I'd have four dead boys on my hands."

"Men," Heck said, "they were men, not boys."

"Whatever they were, two are alive, and two are dead." He glared at Clint.

"Heck kept the young one alive," he said. "We talked him out of going for his gun,"

"Dave's not a bad kid," Wright said, "he just got in with the wrong crowd. That Zack Wyler's always been a troublemaker."

"Wyler's one of the dead ones?" Clint asked.

"From what I heard, he's the one who pushed Dave into the marshal."

"Really too bad he's dead, then, huh?" Heck asked.

"Can I trust you two to go to your hotel?" Wright asked. "Or will I have to invite you to spend the night in jail?"

Clint stood up. For a moment the sheriff didn't know what he had in mind, and he leaned back in his chair.

"We'll go to our hotel, Sheriff," Clint said. "No more trouble tonight. Right, Marshal?"

Heck stood up.

"Right," he said. "No more trouble."

"I don't suppose it would do me any good to ask you for your guns?" the sheriff asked.

"No," Clint said, "no good, at all."

"You can go, then."

"Thanks, Sheriff."

Outside the sheriff's office Heck said, "I'm sorry, Clint."

"For what?"

"On account of me you had to kill two men."

"Yeah, I did," Clint said, "but you saved that boy's life."

"I guess I did."

"Maybe he learned something," Clint said. "Something that'll keep him alive a little while longer."

"Well, I just wanted you to know I'm sorry," Heck said. "I don't usually . . . lose control."

"I know that, Heck," Clint said. "It's understandable, given the way you feel about the Sunday gang."

"The gang," Heck said. "It's Frank Sunday, really. You know, I don't know if he takes a man into his gang and turns him into a bloodthirsty killer, or if he just finds them, but either way once he's gone maybe there'll be a few less killers out there."

"Well," Clint said, "there'll be one, anyway."

They stepped down off the boardwalk and went to their hotel, both men alert for an ambush. Whether it was men Sunday had left behind, or just some drunks on the prod, it seemed as if they had a target drawn on their backs.

They went to their rooms and set up some warning

systems—a pitcher on the windowsill, a chair jammed beneath the doorknob—before undressing and getting into their beds. Both had their gun belts hanging from the bedpost, within easy reach.

It took a while for them to fall asleep, as they both had thoughts spinning in their heads. Clint was wondering if and when Heck Thomas might go off again like he did tonight. It certainly wasn't like him, but he really hadn't seen his friend since he started riding for Judge Parker. Maybe all the years of chasing outlaws was finally getting to him.

For his part Heck Thomas was sifting through the maps he kept in his head, trying to figure out where Frank Sunday was headed so that maybe he and Clint could get there first or, at least, cut him off. Heck knew he had to catch Sunday soon and put an end to this obsession. He didn't need to be told that it wasn't good for him. Losing control had already told him that. The two young men Clint had to kill were a casualty of his need to capture Frank Sunday. He had to end it before there were more.

TWENTY-FIVE

In the morning they checked out of the hotel, had a quick breakfast, then walked over to the livery to collect their horses. From there they stopped at the general store for some supplies, enough so that they could carry them comfortably in their saddlebags and continue to travel light.

When they were loaded up Clint looked at Heck and said, "Ready to go?"

"I done some thinkin' last night," Heck said, as they mounted up.

"About what?"

"We can talk along the way," Heck said. "Let's put this place behind us."

"Don't mind if we do."

They rode toward the west end of town but before they could ride out a figure appeared in the street just ahead of them, legs spread, arms down at his sides.

"Who's that?" Heck asked.

"It's that fool kid from last night," Clint said. "What was his name? McNab."

"Jesus," Heck said, "I guess maybe he didn't learn nothin'."

When they reached Dave McNab they reined in their horses and stared down at him.

"Which one of us you callin' out today, youngster?" Heck asked.

To their surprise instead of adopting a belligerent stance the boy took off his hat and held it in both hands.

"Sirs, I wanted to apologize for last night," he said. "I ain't the smartest person in the world, and I let the drink and my . . . my friends get the better of me. Because of that two of them are dead. Mr. Adams, I'm plumb sorry you had to do that."

"So am I, son."

"You're apology is accepted, boy," Heck said. "No if you'll step aside we'll be on our way."

Abruptly, the boy put his hat back on and held his hands out to them, palms out.

"Please," he said. "I wanna come with you."

"What?" Heck asked.

"I wanna ride with you," McNab said. "I got to get out of this town, Marshal, Mr. Adams."

"Why would we want you to ride with us?" Heck asked.

"I don't know where you're headed," the boy said, "but I bet you could use an extra gun. Marshal, I know you palmed that white poker chip last night. I hit it dead center, didn't I?"

"You did that," Heck replied, "but it's like I said last night, you ain't never stared down a man with the intent of killin' him."

"And, hopefully, you never will," Clint said.

"I think we all know that ain't gonna be the case," Mc-Nab said.

"How's that?" Clint asked.

"The only talent I got is with a gun," McNab said. "That means I got to make my way with it. Sooner or later, that means facing another man with a gun, don't it?"

Clint and Heck exchanged a glance.

"You got a choice in the matter, Dave," Clint said. "You can make the choice right now to put down the gun."

"And do what?" the young man asked. "Work as a clerk in a store?"

"It's honest work," Heck said.

"I'd die," McNab said. "I'd rather be a lawman."

"A lawman?" Heck thought the youngster was on his way to saying he wanted to be a gunman.

"Yes, sir," McNab said. "I figure that's where my talent with a gun could do the most good."

"Look, boy," Heck said. "I'm outta my jurisdiction, and I'm a deputy marshal only by Judge Parker's say so. I got no power to deputize anybody."

"I don't need to be deputized, sir," McNab said. "I just want to ride along with the two of you and learn."

"We ain't teachers," Heck said, "or babysitters."

"I don't need no babysitter!" McNab said, bristling.

"You needed one last night," Heck pointed out.

The boy had no defense for that.

"Marshal, I don't wanna die in this town," McNab said. "I gotta get out."

"So leave," Heck said. "Ain't nobody stoppin' you that I can see. Get on a horse and leave, but you ain't comin' with us."

Heck maneuvered his horse around the boy and headed out of town.

"Can't you talk to him for me, Mr. Adams?" McNab asked desperately. "Please?"

"The marshal's right, Dave," Clint said. "You can't come with us. We're trackin' down a gang of killers."

"But I can help."

"You've got no experience," Clint said. "You're liable to get killed before you can be of any help. Sorry, lad, but I agree with Marshal Thomas. You can leave town, just not with us."

And with that Clint walked Eclipse around the dejected young man and followed Heck Thomas out of town.

TWENTY-SIX

Frank Sunday stared down at the town. It wasn't much of a town, just a few ramshackle wooden buildings to either side of one main street. But it had a name and, more importantly, it had a bank and a saloon.

"Not gonna be much in that bank," said Arch Jackson.

"I just wanna give the boys some exercise," Sunday said. "We'll use the saloon, see if they got a whorehouse, use that. If it don't, we'll just use their women."

"If they have any."

"After that we'll check out their little bank."

The town was called Conway, and was on the border between Texas and Arizona—technically, an Arizona town.

"We ain't that far from where we're goin', Frank," Jackson said. "We could just keep on."

Sunday turned and looked back at the other five men, who sat their horses in a group far enough away so that they couldn't hear the conversation.

"Look," he said to Jackson, "when we get where we're goin' the boys are gonna hafta behave."

"There ain't no law there, Frank," Jackson reminded him.

"That's why, in a split second, lead could be flyin' everywhere," Sunday said. "I wanna lay low, Arch, and I

107

don't want them gettin' into trouble. Tearin' this little town
apart is gonna have to last them a while. Might as well let
'em get their fill while they can."

"Get their fill?" Jackson asked. "From this?"

"It's all we got to give 'em," Sunday said. "I don't
wanna hit a bigger town. That'll come later."

"You're the boss, Frank. Want me to tell 'em?"

"I'll tell 'em," Sunday said. "You wait here, keep
watchin'. Maybe you'll see somethin' important."

About the only thing Arch Johnson could see from the
hill they were on was a few people moving around the
town, a bright dress or two, indicating there were some
women, at least. He knew it didn't matter to the men if the
women were fourteen or forty. Rape was rape, and had
nothing to do with how the woman looked.

Jackson knew that when people talked about the bloodthirsty Sunday gang he always got lumped in with them,
but he wasn't bloodthirsty. Oh, he didn't mind some rapin'
and some killin', but it didn't do for him what it did for
Frank Sunday and the others. Chapman, Henry, Peters,
they came to Frank Sunday with an appetite for it, already.
The other two, Logan and Cuthburt, they learned it from
Frank and the others. Jackson, he was just riding with Sunday, wherever the man led him. That was the way it had
been since they met, and would probably be until the day
one of them died.

Down on that one street Jackson thought he saw something, a glint of metal, maybe off of somebody's chest.

He turned his horse and rode back to tell Sunday there
might be a lawman in town.

Sheriff Mark Alter knew he never should have put on a
badge, but the people of Conway said they needed a sheriff, so less than a year earlier he had accepted the position.
Personally, he didn't know what a town of fifty people
needed with a lawman. Most of them were pretty law-

abiding, and the only trouble he ever had was when some-body drank too much in the town's lone saloon.

So he wore a gun, and a badge, but at thirty-five he was old enough to know that he wasn't a real lawman. He also knew that the day would come when he would have to lay the badge down.

When he saw the seven men riding down the hill to-wards town, he knew they were hell-bent for trouble. He could feel it. And it would be more than getting drunk and shooting up the saloon.

There were only a few people on the street to see him take off his badge, drop it into the dirt, mount the nearest horse and ride out of town.

Conway didn't have a sheriff anymore.

TWENTY-SEVEN

"Gunman's Crossing?" Clint asked. "I thought that was a myth."

"Oh, it's a real place, all right," Heck said.

"And this is what you came up with after all your thinking last night?" Clint asked. "That they're heading for Gunman's Crossing?"

"I said they could be headin' there," Heck replied. "They're goin' in that direction."

"Wait a minute." Clint put his hand out and touched Heck's arm, halting their progress. "You know where Gunman's Crossing is?"

"It's in Arizona."

"What if they're heading for California?" Clint asked. "Or they change direction and go to Colorado?"

"I'm just makin' a guess here, Clint," Heck said. "They've been raidin' and killin' for months."

"And you think everybody needs a break?"

"I know Frank Sunday, Clint," Heck said. "He's a smart man. He'll know when it's time to lay low, and Gunman's Crossing is the place to do it."

"Tell me something," Clint said. "How do you know where this place is?"

Heck hesitated, then said, "I was there, once. It was years ago and I wasn't wearin' a badge then."

"How did you find it?"

"Stumbled on it."

"How many years ago?"

Heck shrugged.

"Fifteen, maybe."

"And you think it's still there?"

"From what I hear, yeah."

Clint leaned back in his saddle.

"Well, I must be out of the loop. Hell, I haven't heard anyone even say that name in years."

"Well," Heck said, "it's out there."

"So what do you suggest?"

"I don't think we can get there ahead of them," Heck said, "so we might as well just head for it ourselves."

"What about their tracks? What if they veer off, away from Gunman's Crossing?"

"Then I'm wrong," Heck said, "and we keep followin' them."

"Do you even know the way to Gunman's Crossing?"

"I guess we're gonna find out."

It was days later when they topped a rise and were able to look down at the remnants of what was once a small town. There were still tendrils of smoke wafting up from the rubble—not enough to have been seen from far off, but enough to know that this destruction had been recent.

"Damn," Heck said.

"Yeah."

"We better ride down and see if anyone's left," Heck said. "They might need help."

This was a change from Heck's former attitude, which would have been to skirt the town and continue on in pursuit of Frank Sunday and his gang.

"Might have to bury the dead, Heck."

"Let's hope enough of them survived to bury their own dead."

They started down the hill.

As they approached what was left of Conway, Arizona, they could smell the burning flesh. Unfortunately, it was an odor they both knew well and had hoped never to encounter again.

There hadn't been many buildings to begin with, and now there wasn't one still standing as a whole. There was a leaning wall on one side of the street, and a section of a building that had survived the flames on the other. They rode to the center of town and dismounted.

"Take the other side of the street," Heck said. "Call out if you find anybody alive."

"Right."

There were the burnt-out remnants of three or four buildings on the other side of the street. Clint got as close to them as he could. For the most part the fires had burnt out days ago. He wasn't sure what they'd seen from the hill, but at the moment there was no smoke. There were, however, plenty of bodies, most of them burnt to a crisp. He found several bodies outside one building, and they had been shot several times. He stepped on something and looked down to see that it was a sign that said BANK OF CONWAY.

He stepped into the rubble, walked carefully so as not to step on any bodies. In the back he found a safe, which was open and empty. How much, he wondered, could a town of this size have had in their safe?

"Clint?"

He turned and saw Heck standing just outside. He turned and walked back to join him.

"Anybody on your side of the street?" he asked.

"No," Heck said. "Doesn't look much better here, either."

"I found some bodies outside," Clint said, "but most are

in the buildings, burned up. Apparently, this was their bank."

"The tracks I found were made by the Sunday gang," Heck said. "I doubt they stopped here to hit the bank. My guess is they meant to burn the town to the ground and kill everybody in it. The bank might have been an afterthought."

"So, just another day in the life of the Sunday gang, huh?" Clint asked.

"I found some women across the street," Heck said. "Raped, and then killed. So yeah, I'd say that was true."

They stood there amidst the rubble, as if taking a moment of silence for the town.

"Let's mount up and take a ride around. Maybe there's somebody alive on the outskirts."

Clint looked down at kicked at the bank sign.

"If they hear us coming they might just hide," Clint said. "They don't have much cause to trust strangers."

Both men started across the street to the horses when Clint felt something under his boot. He stopped and bent to pick it up.

"What is it?" Heck asked.

Clint held it out in the palm of his hand. It was a silver sheriff's badge. It hadn't been torn off. It looked as if someone had simply unpinned it and dropped it in the dirt.

"Let's hope that poor bastard got away alive," Heck said.

Clint nodded. He was about to drop the badge back into the dirt, but for some reason stuck it in his pocket, instead.

TWENTY-EIGHT

After making a slow circuit of the town and its environs Clint and Heck were about to ride away, convinced that everyone who had been in town was dead. But before they could they thought they heard someone calling out to them. They both turned in their saddles and saw someone running towards them—someone who had come over a second hill, south of town.

"Wait," the man was yelling. "Wait."

"Survivor," Clint said.

"Maybe," Heck said. "We better be careful. It just might be an ambush."

They gigged their horses and rode towards the approaching figure. As they got closer they saw it was a man wearing a gun.

"That's far enough," Heck called out, drawing his gun. "Stop right there."

The man did as he was told.

"Hands away from your body."

The man spread his hands.

"Who are you?"

"My name is Mark Alter," the man said. "I am—or was—the sheriff of Conway."

"Prove it," Heck said. "Where's your badge?"

"I . . . I took it off and dropped it in the street."

"Why?"

"I saw the riders coming," Alter said. "I was going to run."

"What changed your mind?"

"They rode into town and started shooting right away," Alter said. "I had to come back."

"To do what?" Clint asked. "You couldn't fight seven of them."

Alter turned and looked behind him. Several figures were coming down the hill, the way he had just come.

"I had to save as many of the children as I could," he said.

Clint and Heck noticed that the approaching figures were, indeed, children and they were of various ages.

"How many?" Clint asked.

"Eight," Alter said. "Ages five through fourteen. Their parents are all dead."

"Do they know that?"

"Yes, they do."

"They should know that you had no choice," Clint said. "If you had tried to stop the gang alone they would have killed you."

"They know that," Alter said. "They don't blame me."

"And what about you?" Heck asked, lowering his gun. "Do you know that?"

"In my heart I do," Alter said, "but . . ."

"Can't forgive yourself, can you?" Clint asked.

The man shook his head.

"No, I can't."

Clint dug into his pocket and came out with the discarded badge.

"I think this is yours." He held it out to the man.

Alter came forward and accepted the badge, looked at it sadly.

"Doesn't much matter, does it?" he asked. "There is no Conway left to be sheriff of."

Clint and Heck couldn't argue with that. The children reached them and crowded around Alter. The youngest was a girl, the oldest a boy she was clinging to. In all, four girls, four boys.

"Were there other children in town?" Clint asked.

"Some," Alter said, pinning his badge back on. "There were several teenage girls."

Clint and Heck had seen what the gang did with teenage girls.

"I couldn't get to them in time."

"What's the nearest town?" Clint asked.

"Trinity," Alter said. "It's a couple of miles that way." He pointed north.

"We can take you," Clint said. "Some of you."

"Are you tracking that gang?"

"We are," Heck said.

"Then no," Alter said. "We can walk. Don't lose their trail."

Heck holstered his gun, exchanged a glance with Clint.

"All right," he said. "Wait here."

Clint and Heck took out what stores they had left, some dried beef and canned peaches, mostly. They also handed over a canteen of water, kept one for themselves.

"Sorry it can't be more," Clint said.

"It's only a couple of miles," Alter said, again. "We'll make it just fine."

"We're sorry about your town," Heck said, "your people."

"Not your fault."

"We could have caught them sooner," Heck said, "prevented all this."

"Maybe," Alter said, "maybe not, but if I'm not gonna blame myself, then you fellas have to do the same."

Clint rode forward and shook the man's hand.

"You saved these children," he said. "You accomplished a lot when you could have just kept running."

"I'm ashamed I even thought about it."

"You're only human," Heck said.

He and Clint turned their horses and headed east. Sheriff Mark Alter called out after them, "You just get those bastards!"

"We will," Heck Thomas said. "I promise you, we will."

TWENTY-NINE

They followed the tracks of the Sunday gang through Arizona for a few days, until they headed north. At that point they camped and discussed what their next move should be.

"They're either headed for Colorado," Heck said, "or they're goin' to Gunman's Crossing."

"Both are north of here?"

"Yes."

"Well, can't we just stay on their trail and find out?"

"Here's the thing," Heck said, putting down his plate of beans so he could gesture with his hands. "There are two ways to get into Gunman's Crossing. It looks to me like if that's where they're going, they're gonna go in the front way."

"And there's a back way?"

"Yes."

"And you've gone in that way?"

"I told you, I stumbled into the place," Heck said. "I didn't mean to go there, but I did."

"Where is this place?"

"It's in a canyon below the Colorado Plateau," Heck said. "If we go that way from here, we can beat them there."

"If that's where they're headed."

'Right."

"And if that back way hasn't somehow been closed off."

"Right."

"And if it has been closed off?"

"Then one of two things happens."

"What's that?"

"We either come back and pick up their trail again."

"Or?"

Heck picked up his beans again and said, "Or we give up. We'll lose 'em."

Clint sat back on his rock, ate his beans and gave it some thought for a while.

"Are you willing to do that?" he finally asked. "Take a chance on losing them?"

"I think it's a good bet."

"And you'd give up then? Go back to the Territories? After chasing them this far?"

"It makes sense to me that Gunman's Crossing is where they're goin'," Heck said.

"And not . . . say, Denver."

"Denver's too big for them," Heck said. "They're vicious, small-time killers, Clint. Denver would never even occur to them. And Frank has never given me any indication he'd be comfortable in the mountains. No, I think Gunman's Crossing is as close to Colorado as they'll get."

Clint studied Heck. His friend seemed to have passed through that desperate phase and come out the other side. Maybe the shooting in Tucumcari had helped him through it, but he no longer seemed to have a fever to catch Frank Sunday behind his eyes. No he seemed calm and collected.

"It's your call, Heck," Clint said. "Whichever way you decide to go, I'll follow you."

Heck chewed, nodded and said again, "Seems a good bet to me."

"I'll make my wager with you, then."

• • •

They still split a watch that night, even though they felt that
the Sunday gang was well ahead of them. In the morning
Clint had the last watch so he made a pot of coffee. For
breakfast they ate the last of their beef jerky.

"We're short of supplies," Clint said. "If we're going to
Gunman's Crossing we'll need to pick some up someplace."

"There's a small trading post up ahead," Heck said, "before we leave the road to head into the canyon the back
way."

"Wow, what a memory," Clint said. "You can remember
from that far back that there was a trading post?"

"Well," Heck said, "that and I saw a sign a few miles
back that said Trading Post."

Clint was surprised at how much more relaxed Heck
seemed than he had been for most of the trip.

"You're back in lawman mode," he said.

"What?"

"You're acting and thinking like a lawman again," Clint
said, "and not like somebody with a personal interest."

"Ah," Heck said, "after Tucumcari I decided I'd probably get you killed unless I pulled myself together."

"Well, I appreciate it."

Heck nodded and held his coffee cup out. Clint poured
it full, then emptied the pot into his own cup. He was never
a one to waste good trail coffee on dousing a fire—and he
considered that he made good trail coffee. He'd stomp the
fire out when they were done.

"So what do you want to do about the kid?" he asked
Heck.

"He's still out there, ain't he?"

"Yup."

"I was wonderin' if you noticed," Heck said.

"I noticed, back before we even got to Conway."

"He's not very good at shadowing us."

"Maybe he wanted to be seen," Clint said. "Maybe he's

been wanting us to call him into camp for some hot food and coffee."

"Yeah, seems he's been making cold camp pretty much every night," Heck said.

"Well, what are our options with this kid?" Clint wondered aloud.

"Well, we can let him follow us into Gunman's Crossing," Heck said. "He'll probably do somethin' there to get us all killed."

"Or?"

"Or we can shoo him off."

"How do we do that?"

"I don't know," Heck said. "Shoot him?"

"We can't shoot him."

"Shoot at him?"

"I don't think that would work," Clint said. "He seems pretty determined."

"Well then, I'll suggest shooting him just one more time."

"We can't shoot him, Heck."

"Well then I'm done," Heck said. "You don't like my ideas, you decide what to do with him."

"Well, we can try scaring him."

"How do we do that?"

"Call him in, tell him where we're going," Clint said. "Maybe it'll frighten him off."

"And if it don't?" Heck asked.

"Hell, we'll take him with us."

"What?"

"Sure," Clint said. "At least then we can keep an eye on him, keep him from doing something stupid."

"We could send him in the front way," Heck said. "Use him as a decoy. Distract everyone's attention from our arrival."

"Everyone's?"

"Well, it's a town," Heck said. "May not have any law,

but they'll have a saloon, and a bank, and some stores. It's a damn town, Clint. What did you think it was? It's got a name and everything. So if he goes in first, a stranger riding in alone, it would be a distraction."

"I thought you were done coming up with ideas."

"It just occurred to me."

"Well, that'd get him killed for sure," Clint said.

"And that'd be a distraction."

"Heck . . ."

"Hell, then call him in," Heck said. "Let's talk to him and see how all-fired determined he really is."

"Okay," Clint said, "okay, I'll call him in—but first I'll make another pot of coffee."

THIRTY

"How did you know I was out there?" the kid asked after he'd ridden into camp.

"Kid," Clint said, "you're not very good at following people. You've got to learn to keep your horse quiet, and watch where you step."

"Hey," McNab said, "maybe I'm not so good at following somebody without them knowing it, but I followed the two of you this far, didn't I?"

"He's got you there, Clint," Heck said.

Clint handed Dave McNab a cup of coffee.

"We've got no more food," he said, apologetically. "We finished the last of our jerky."

"I've still got some," McNab said. He fished a couple of pieces out of his pocket and handed them across to Clint and Heck.

"Thanks," Heck said.

"I didn't give mine up to those kids in Conway like you did," he explained.

"Let me tell you why we decided to wave you in," Clint said.

"I'm listenin'."

Clint explained what they were doing, and the various ways the kid could take part in their plan. To his credit McNab listened intently without interrupting.

"So," Clint finished, "what do you say?"

"I'll go in with the two of you," he answered without hesitation.

"Why?" Heck asked.

"Because it's the way I'll learn the most."

"How do you figure?" Clint asked.

"Well, if I turn back I won't learn nothin'," the kid said. "If I go in alone, the front way, I'm dead, and I won't learn nothin', either." He shrugged. "That only leaves goin' with you."

Clint looked at Heck, who shrugged and said, "Sounds logical to me."

Clint looked at McNab.

"If you're coming with us you have to do exactly as you're told, without question."

"How about if—" the kid started to ask, but Clint cut him off.

"I just said without question."

McNab closed his mouth.

"Do you understand?"

"Yes, sir."

"Okay, then," Clint said. "Since you're already saddled you break camp while Heck and I saddle our horses. And make damn sure the fire is out."

"Yes, sir."

Clint and Heck walked over to where their horses were picketed and began saddling them.

"What do you think?" Clint asked.

"I think he's got his logic down pretty good," Heck said. "And we saw in the saloon that he can handle a gun."

"Yeah," Clint said, "shooting at glasses and poker chips. He's untested facing another man."

"I guess it's gonna be up to us to see that he passes his first test," Heck said.

"And if he doesn't," Clint added, "one of us might just end up dead."

When they had their horses saddled they tied their bedrolls on, and replaced their saddlebags. They had one canteen between them because they'd given one to Sheriff Alter for him and the kids.

They walked their horses back to where McNab had stomped the fire out and used the last of the coffee to douse the embers for good. Clint could see he was going to have to teach the kid about good trail coffee and its uses. The kid had apparently stowed the coffee pot in his own saddlebags.

"Ready to go?" Clint asked.

"I'm more than ready."

"We'll ride single file with you in the back," Clint said. "Heck will take the lead because he knows where we're going."

"Sorta," Heck added.

"Sort of?" the kid asked.

"It's a long story," Clint said. "Just stay behind me and watch our backs. If you see anybody behind us sing out."

"Ain't the gang we're trackin' in front of us?"

"That don't mean somebody might not double back behind us," Heck told him. "Understand?"

"Yes, sir."

"Mount up," Clint said.

"Yes, sir."

"Wait a minute."

McNab looked at him.

"When's the last time you cleaned your weapons?"

"Last night," McNab said. "When I camped . . . and the night before, too."

"Twice in two nights?" Heck asked.

"I kicked up a lot of dust following you guys," he said. "I wanted to make sure they'd work if I needed them."

Clint looked at Heck, who shrugged.

"Besides," the kid added with a shrug, "I didn't have nothin' else to do."

THIRTY-ONE

Once again Frank Sunday and Arch Jackson sat their horses ahead of the other five men, who were clustered together yards behind them.

"Whataya think, Frank?"

"I don't know, Arch," Sunday said. "Denver? What would we do in Denver?"

"Same thing we'd do in Gunman's Crossing," Jackson said. "Lay low."

"In Denver?" Sunday asked. "You really think those five could stay out of trouble in a big city?"

"Well, I—"

"Hell, you really think we could stay out of trouble in Denver?" Sunday asked, cutting Jackson off. "No, Gunman's Crossing is the place for us."

Arch Jackson looked North, toward Colorado and Denver.

"Hey Arch," Sunday said, "you wanna go to Denver, be my guest. We'll lay low at the Crossing and meet you later."

"No," Jackson said, "I'll stick with you, Frank . . . like I always do."

Sunday slapped Jackson on the back.

"Besides," Sunday said, "you know those five. They like

to burn down every town they stay in. Can you imagine them tryin' to burn down Denver?"

Jackson didn't say a word about how he'd once read that a cow had almost burned down Chicago. He didn't know if they had any cows in Denver.

Hank Chapman, Dylan Henry, Larry Peters, Sam Logan, and Dennis Cuthbert watched as Frank Sunday and Arch Jackson had their private discussion.

"How come we never get to vote on where we go next?" Henry asked the others.

"Hey," Chapman said, "be my guest. You go and tell those two where ya wanna go."

"Yeah," Cuthbert said, with a laugh, "go and tell 'em that. I wanna see."

"I'm just sayin'," Henry responded, "it'd be nice if we got a say-so once in a while."

"Hey," Logan said, "we're in the Sunday gang. I don't have no problem with Frank always bein' the one to say where we go. We been doin' pretty good."

"Nobody's sayin' we ain't," Henry said. "It was just a comment, is all."

"My suggestion," Chapman said to Henry, "would be to keep your damn comments to yerself."

"Gunman's Crossing is good enough for me," Larry Peters said. "I ain't never been there. Any of you ever been there?"

"I was there once," Chapman said.

"What's it like?" Peters asked.

"A town, like any other town," Chapman said. "A saloon, a bank, a hotel . . ."

"A lawman?" Sam Logan asked.

"I tell ya what, they got a jail house, but no lawman."

"Whores?" Cuthbert asked.

"Lots of whores, Dennis," Chapman said, "and you ain't got to pay 'em."

"Wait a minute," Dylan Henry said. "The whores lay with you for free?"

"Well, no," Chapman said, "they don't charge ya, but ya gotta tip 'em."

"Tip a whore?" Henry said. "Hell, if a whore gives me a poke and don't charge me, I ain't givin' her a red cent."

"That's why whores don't like you, Dylan," Cuthburt said. "Yer cheap."

"You better shut—"

"We all better shut up," Chapman said. "Here they come."

Sunday and Jackson came riding back and Frank Sunday said, "Boys, we're goin' on to Gunman's Crossing."

"They got whores there, Frank?" Dylan Henry asked. "Chapman says they got whores ya don't gotta pay."

"He says ya gotta tip 'em," Sam Logan said.

"If you don't tip a whore in Gunman's Crossing," Sunday said, "you better never go back to her. You'll wake up and find her with a bloody knife in one hand and your dick in the other."

"Jeez—" Henry said, as that picture formed in his mind.

"Listen, boys," Sunday said, "ya gotta behave in Gunman's Crossing, ya know? If one of us gets in trouble they'll kick all of us out. And we don't want that."

"How long we gotta stay there, Frank?" Henry asked.

"Until I decide it's time ta go," Sunday said. "We just gotta let the heat die down on us a little, that's all."

"What about that marshal?" Cuthburt asked. "You think he's still comin'?"

"Oh, he's comin', all right," Sunday said. "I want him to follow us right into the Crossing. You know what Gunman's Crossing is for a lawman?"

Nobody did, so he grinned and said, "Hell on earth, boys. Hell on earth."

THIRTY-TWO

"You sure he knows where he's takin' us?" Dave McNab whispered to Clint Adams.

"He knows," Clint said, totally unsure, himself. "He was there once before."

"And he got out alive?"

"He wasn't a lawman then," Clint said, "and yeah, he got out alive."

Heck Thomas was just ahead of them, standing in his stirrups, examining the terrain.

"You sure we ain't lost?" McNab asked.

"We're not lost, Dave," Clint said. "Heck will find the way."

Heck turned his horse and came back to them.

"How we doin'?" Clint asked hopefully.

"Oh, it's out there," Heck said.

"Yeah, but are we gonna find it?" McNab asked.

Heck glared at the kid.

"Don't worry, I'll find it," he said. "You can always turn around and head back, ya know."

"No," McNab said, "I'll stick with you, Marshal."

"And that's another thing."

"What?" the kid asked.

"The one thing you have to remember about Gunman's Crossing is that usually people there mind their own business. Oh, there are disputes and men handle 'em the way men handle 'em, but the one thing they all have in common is that they hate lawmen. A lawman in there, once he's discovered, is as good as dead."

"But . . . you're a lawman," McNab said.

"That's right," Heck said, 'but you got to forget that."

"Forget it?" McNab screwed up his face, puzzled.

"Kid," Clint said, "stop calling him marshal. It'll get him killed, for sure."

"Oh," McNab said, "right. Okay, Mar—uh, I mean . . ."

"Just call me Heck."

"Yes, sir . . . Heck."

"Now let's get rollin'," Heck sad. "We need to find a good place to camp, and then tomorrow we'll ride into the Crossing."

"Yes, sir, Mar—uh, I mean, Heck."

"You ride drag again," Heck said to him. "I'll take point—and mind where your horse steps. We ain't gonna be on any kind of road from here on out."

"Got it."

Heck looked at Clint and when the boy wasn't watching rolled his eyes.

Ten men sat around two campfires that night, all headed for the same place, all with different ideas of what was going to happen when they got there. In the outlaw camp they built two fires. Frank Sunday and Arch Jackson sat around one, while the other five men sat around the other.

Frank Sunday had some extra cash in one of his saddlebags that nobody but Jackson knew about. When you rode into Gunman's Crossing and you intended to stay a while you had to pay a fee. If you were just passing through the fee was waived. And when you rode in with a gang and were going to stay you had to pay so much per head. Since the men followed him, Sunday felt it was his duty to pay for each of them.

Once they settled down each man would be on his own and pay his own way. Also, any man who got into a dispute would have to settle it on his own. Sunday would not risk his own life backing anyone's play, unless it was Arch Jackson, and he knew his *segundo* felt the same way. If the other boys wanted to get into a fight they'd be on their own as far as he and Jackson were concerned. If they wanted to back each other's play, that was also up to them.

Sunday's expectations for Gunman's Crossing was to spend some time gambling, some time eating, some time with women, and some time by himself. When he felt he was sufficiently relaxed, and that things had cooled down enough, then he and the gang would leave the Crossing and start up operations again. And there was also one other thing that had to be done.

He had to kill Heck Thomas. He was the only lawman who wouldn't just forget about the gang once they passed out of his jurisdiction. He didn't need some crazy lawman on his tail who didn't honor boundaries. Frank Sunday liked lawmen who took off their badges when they went home at night, and pinned it back on in the morning when they went to work. He swore Heck Thomas must've pinned his badge on his pajamas when he went to sleep at night.

Crazy man, that's what he was.

Arch Jackson regarded Frank Sunday across the fire. Behind him he could hear the others jawing away, laughing or grumbling at each other. Before long the paste boards would come out and they'd start playing poker. Few words passed between him and Sunday when they were around the campfire. Sometimes Sunday wanted his opinion about something, but usually the gang leader made up his own mind about things.

Once they were in Gunman's Crossing Jackson was determined to set his *segundo* role aside. He'd see to his own

needs in town and stay out of trouble unless he had to back
a play of Sunday's—but that wasn't likely. He knew that
Sunday had the same intentions he had; just to relax, settle
down some, spend some quiet time. Arch Jackson knew,
though, that one thing would be on both his mind and
Frank Sunday's while they were there.

Deputy Marshal Heck Thomas.

There was no way they'd be able to leave Gunman's
Crossing and start up again with him on their trail. If Frank
Sunday was right Heck Thomas would follow them into
Gunman's Crossing, where they'd be able to kill him with
no repercussions. The Crossing was about the only place
you could get away with killing a lawman. And Jackson
wasn't like Sunday. Frank wanted to kill the marshal himself. Jackson didn't care who killed him, as long as he was
dead and off their trail.

But Jackson knew he was putting more thought into it
than Sunday was. For instance . . . what if Thomas didn't
come alone? And if he wasn't alone, who'd be with him?
Other lawmen riding out of their jurisdiction? Some Arizona lawman who'd taken up with him? Or just some
friends of his who wore no badges, but who would back his
play. Whenever he brought the question up to Sunday he
always got the same answer.

"It don't matter," he said. "We'll be in the Crossing.
We'll take care of him and whoever he brings with him."

Arch Jackson had found that Frank Sunday was usually
right. He hoped the same would be true, this time.

Heck Thomas stood first watch and noticed something. For
the first time in days—maybe weeks—he couldn't hear his
own heart pounding in his ears. He'd been aware of it ever
since his decision to pursue the Sunday gang to hell and
back, if he needed to. He knew that he was intent on bring-
ing the Sunday gang to justice—one way or another—to
the detriment of every other aspect of his life. In fact for

the past few weeks or months the only thing he concentrated on was that gang—no, not even the gang. It was Frank Sunday, himself. It consumed him and became the only reason his heart beat every day. And so he became aware of that beat as it was constantly in his ears.

But the incident in Tucumcari, where they'd met Dave McNab, and where Clint Adams had been forced to kill two drunken young men, seemed to have calmed his heart beat. Up to that point he felt like nothing more than a tea pot with water inside and heat underneath waiting for the steam to explode from the spout. And he thought that when it exploded it would be a bad thing, but that incident seemed to have allowed the steam to leak out without an explosion. Now he was back to being the lawman he always was, calm, determined, not as manic as he had been about catching this gang.

Oh, he was still determined to catch Frank Sunday, just not as feverish. And with Clint Adams backing his play he felt they were more than a match for Frank Sunday, Arch Jackson, and the rest. And maybe the kid, McNab, even gave them a small edge.

He also knew that as the only lawman among the three of them his life would not be worth a plugged nickel in the Crossing if that fact became known. They were going to have to get in and out with Sunday and his gang—or, at the very least, with Frank Sunday—before the rest of the desperados in that town found out he was a marshal.

For that to happen, they were going to need a pretty damn good plan.

Clint also knew they needed a pretty damn good plan. He was rolled up in his bedroll, the kid snoring somewhere off to his right. As he stared at the sky he knew that while all their lives were on the line, the one who was most at risk was Heck Thomas. If the denizens of Gunman's Crossing found out he was the law, Heck was as good as dead—and most likely, them with him.

In order to get in there and get out again with Frank
Sunday and any members of his gang, it was going to take
more than sheer gunplay. It was going to take planning.

He watched as Heck Thomas dropped another handful
of coffee grounds into the campfire pot. Heck made pass-
able trail coffee, and Clint decided that since he couldn't
sleep he'd get up and have some, and maybe talk out a plan
with his friend that would get them all out of Gunman's
Crossing alive.

A plan, he thought as he got to his feet, or a goddamn
miracle.

THIRTY-THREE

It took until mid-afternoon for Heck Thomas to finally find a point of reference for himself.

"There," he said. "That rock formation. See it?"

"Looks like a big finger pointing up," Dave McNab said.

"A big, craggy finger," Clint said, "but a finger."

"I remember that," Heck said. "We're on the right track."

"This place seems to have been easier to find when you just stumbled into it," Clint observed.

"It was," Heck said. "Lucky for me I wasn't wearin' a badge back then. I was able to get something to eat, stay overnight and get out without any trouble."

"No trouble at all?" McNab asked. "In Gunman's Crossing?" Even a youngster like him had heard the stories.

"Oh, there were a couple of shootings, one in the street and one in the saloon, but I wasn't involved."

"Only one saloon?" McNab asked.

"Back then, yes," Heck said. "I'll bet they've got a couple more by now."

"So how far do you think we are now?" Clint asked. The sun was high above them and they had run out of water.

"Not far," Heck said. "I can smell the cold beer now."

Clint hoped his friend was telling the truth. With no food and no water and the horses starting to stagger a bit, he didn't know how much longer they could go on. He had to say one thing for the kid, though. He kept up and never complained.

They came around a sharp bend an hour later and Heck said, "There it is."

Clint saw it. It was a town, all right. They were looking at the back of a row of buildings.

"I can already see how it's grown," Heck said. "When I was here there was just that one single row of buildings."

From their vantage point Clint could see that the available points of entry to them were two alleyways.

"Looks like nobody's ever thought of closing off this back way in," Clint said.

"Maybe nobody's found it since I did," Heck said.

"Maybe," Clint said.

"Can we ride in now?" the kid asked. "Heck said he could smell the beer a while back. Well, now I can taste it."

"One thing before we go in," Clint said.

"What's that?" Heck asked.

"You better do something about that badge," Clint said, "before it gets us all killed."

"Oh, right."

Heck removed it and shoved it into a vest pocket.

"I've got another suggestion," he said.

"What's that?"

"Three riders together might attract too much attention."

"I can ride in alone," McNab offered.

"No," Heck said. "A kid your age riding in alone might also get some attention."

"What do you suggest?" Clint asked, although he thought he knew what his friend was getting at.

"You two ride in together," Heck said. "I'll wait here about an hour and ride in after you."

Clint knew that Heck wanted to ride in alone just in case there was someone in town who recognized him. With Clint and McNab going in first they wouldn't be connected to him. Even if he drew fire and got himself killed, they'd be safe. From that point on they could continue after the Sunday gang, or ride out and save their own hides. It wouldn't matter to Heck Thomas.

He'd be dead.

THIRTY-FOUR

Clint and Dave McNab rode down one of the alleys, expecting to come out onto a busy town street. Instead, what they found was a deserted street.

"What the—" Clint said.

They looked both ways, then rode out into the center of the street and stopped there. There was no movement anywhere. Nothing.

"A ghost town?" McNab asked. "Is that what Gunman's Crossing is?"

"That's what it looks like," Clint said.

There were several buildings on each side of the street, all looking as if they'd seen better days. The street dead-ended on one side against a rock wall. Going the other way it seemed to curve out of sight.

"What do we do?" McNab asked.

"Well . . ." At first Clint was going to suggest they follow the street but just then he spotted something. "Come this way."

He directed his horse over to one of the buildings, with McNab behind him. Above the entrance was a faded sign that said DOLLAR BILL'S HOTEL.

"What are we doin' here?" McNab asked.

"Thought I saw some movement inside."

He dismounted and McNab followed. Together they entered the hotel, found themselves in a small lobby that was remarkably clean. They were still looking around when a man came through a curtained doorway behind the desk.

"Oh," he said, "guests." He wiped his hands on his trouser legs, then put them on top of the desk. He seemed to be in his sixties, but could have been even older than that. "Can I help you?"

"Are you . . . open for business?" Clint asked.

"Oh, yes," the man said. "We're the only business still operating at this end of town."

"This end?"

"The new section is around the curve in the street," the clerk said.

"Ah," Clint said, "so this isn't Gunman's Crossing?"

"It used to be," the clerk said. "Now they just call this the old section."

"And the new section is now Gunman's Crossing?"

"Bigger and better," the man said, "but still Gunman's Crossing."

"And still lawless?" McNab asked.

"Decidedly," the man said. "My name is Simon Handler. You gents want a room?"

Clint and McNab were standing out in front of the hotel when Heck Thomas finally came riding in. They could see that he, too, was surprised at the condition of the street— probably more so than they were. They waved until he saw them and rode over to them.

"What the hell happened?" he asked.

"They built a new section of town and everyone moved there except this hotel," Clint said.

Heck looked up at the name of the place.

"This is where I stayed when I was here last."

"We took rooms here," McNab said. "One for you, too."

"You can put your horse around back," Clint said. "We thought this would be easier. We can walk to the other end of town instead of riding in. We'll attract much less attention that way."

"Good thinkin'." Heck dismounted. "Dave, will you take my horse around back for me?'

"Sure, Marsh—I mean, sure, Heck."

He handed the reins to the boy, who walked the horse over to an alley that led to the back of the hotel. Clint and Heck went inside.

"Jesus, this hasn't changed much," Heck said.

"'Afternoon, good sir," the clerk said.

Heck stared at the man, then at Clint.

"He greeted me the same way last time," he said. "Wow, he *has* changed."

"Gunman's Crossing seems to have grown quite a bit since you were here last, Heck, but one thing stayed the same according to the clerk. Still no law."

"Wonder why they didn't just tear this section down?" Heck said, aloud.

"Mr. Handler there—the clerk and owner—says that the last business just moved out last week. He's the only one left. He's afraid they're going to come and burn him out any day."

"Why doesn't he leave?"

"He says he's seventy-four. Where would he go? I think if they came and burned this place down he'd just stay and burn with it."

"Poor old guy."

"He keeps the rooms as clean as this lobby," Clint said. "He says there are two new, big hotels in the new section of town that aren't as clean as this one."

'I'll bet."

McNab appeared at the front door, carrying Heck's rifle and saddlebags.

"I better put these in my room," Heck said, "and then

we can go and take a look at the new section of town. I'll bet we'll be able to find a good meal."

"We'll wait for you here," Clint said.

Heck nodded. Clint gave him his key and he and McNab went out onto the front walk while Heck went to his room.

"Listen," McNab said.

They stood still and heard piano music coming from around the bend.

"Saloons are starting up," Clint said.

"They're gonna be full of outlaws on the prod, ain't they?" the kid asked.

"No," Clint said, "they'll be full of outlaws trying to lay low for a while. There may be a few looking for a fight, Dave, but for the most part they're going to want to mind their own business."

The boy wiped his palms on his thighs.

"Nervous?" Clint asked.

McNab looked at him. For a moment Clint thought he might lie but then the young man said, "Yeah, I am."

"Good," Clint said. "In fact, you should be downright scared. This is important, Dave, so listen good."

"I'm listenin'."

"You don't go for your gun unless Heck or I do. Got it? I know you're nervous, and you're going to be jumpy, but don't make any mistakes. It'll get us all killed. You follow our lead."

"Yes, sir."

Heck came walking out and said, "Are we ready?"

Clint looked at McNab.

"We ready, kid?"

McNab licked his lips and said, "we're ready."

THIRTY-FIVE

They decided to walk to the new section of town, and leave their horses where they were. Simon Handler told them that no one really came to the old part anymore, so their animals should be safe. He also promised to check on them.

As they walked up the street and into the curve of the street the new part of town suddenly presented itself to them. It began with a large livery stable and then stretched out on both sides of the street.

"I never expected a whole damn town," Heck said.

The buildings looked new and the smell of fresh cut wood was still in the air. He wondered if there was a mayor, and a town council, even if there wasn't law. What if this had turned into a true town, and not the lawless hide-out it was rumored to be? Except that Simon Handler had told them that there was still no law here.

"How can you have a town with no law?" Dave McNab said, out loud.

"That's a good question," Clint said. "Let's get up on the boardwalk and stop standing in the middle of the street, gaping."

There were people walking the street, men and women

147

going about their business. What was missing was the traf-
fic that would normally have been provided by local
ranches and/or farms. Buckboards coming to town for supplies, ranch hands riding in for some recreation. But with
no ranches in the area, the streets were relatively clear.
There were no ruts cut into it by the constant influx of
buckboards and wagons and stagecoaches.

The piano music was much clearer from where they
stood now. They could see men going through batwing
doors part way down the street. Just from where they stood
they saw three saloons.

"I'll tell you what else is missing," Heck said, as if read-
ing their minds.

"What's that?" Clint asked.

"Shots," Heck said. "Last time I was here there was always shots being fired."

"Maybe there's no lawmen to uphold the law as we
know it," Clint said, "but there are rules."

"You got rules," Heck said, "you need somebody to en-
force them."

"That's right."

"Well, we got to make sure we don't break any rules
while we're here," Heck told them, then added, "not until
we're good and ready, anyway."

"At the moment," Clint said, "all I want is a cold beer.
Let's mosey over to the smallest saloon we can find—"

"Or the biggest," Heck cut in.

"You have a point," Clint said. "We can blend in better
in the biggest one."

"Looks like that one over there fits the bill," Heck said.

"Well, lead the way," Clint said. "Badge or no badge
you're still the boss."

Gunman's Crossing had come a long way over the years. It
was the brainchild of a man named Victor Cannon. He and
his gang had been looking for a place to lay low twenty

years ago and had come across a forgotten Arizona town. He referred to it as forgotten because the people had not been gone long enough for it to become a ghost town. The buildings were still in good shape, and any signs indicating what the town might have been called were gone. He and his five men had found some supplies left behind in the general store that had probably been too much for the people to carry away with them, and enough whiskey in the saloon to last them. They started using the place as a regular hideout, and even offered it to other gangs as a place to lay low. Each time they returned they brought more supplies with them, and finally Cannon started leaving a man or two behind to try to maintain the place. Soon other gangs came in his absence and he realized that if they had a hotel as well as a saloon, and maybe a restaurant, they could make some money while providing fellow outlaws a place to relax, with no law to worry about. Eventually the place became a going concern and he knew he had to name it. Gunman's Crossing came to him right away.

The Crossing became a place of legend. Outlaws knew of it, lawmen had heard the stories, but most didn't believe it. There had even been a couple of dime novels written about it, comparing it to the Hole-in-the-Wall. But for everyone who knew the name of the place, no one knew who had started it, or who ran it.

After twenty years, now with many new buildings and an influx of regulars who ran the local businesses, Victor Cannon, now a robust sixty, still ran the Crossing. He was the unofficial mayor and sheriff, known to the men who worked for him simply as the Boss.

He sat in his new office in what in a normal town would be called the City Hall. Here it had no name, but everyone knew what it housed. If they'd been able to get bricks into the Crossing's canyon it would have been a two-story brick structure, but since that was impossible it was made of wood, like all the others. He'd thought about putting some

sort of fancy façade on it, but decided against it. Why paint
a target on his back by telling people somebody important
was there? He had his office in the front, where he could
overlook the street, and a two room living space in the
back, where he read, slept, and took his women.

He stood in his window now, hands clasped behind him,
staring down at the street. He was wondering—as he'd
been doing lately—if it was time to bring some law to
town, maybe a town council, turn Gunman's Crossing into
a real town? Was that something he wanted to do after all
these years, go legit? And if he did would he then have to
start trying to keep the outlaw element out?

There was still not a wide enough entrance to the
canyon to bring in things like bricks and better building
supplies, or to make the town accessible to normal travel-
ers. Stagecoaches would have a devil of a time getting in.
He'd thought about having expensive furniture from St.
Louis, but it never would have made the trip. No, there was
a reason the town in its original incarnation—whatever it
had been called—had failed. He needed to stop having
delusions of grandeur and just be happy keeping the town
what it was—a haven for outlaws who were willing to pay
for the right to stay there.

He knew this was what made him different from other
men. He recognized that he could start having thoughts of
doing things that were beyond his reach, and he could deal
with that. Lesser men would have become frustrated, unhappy with their lot in life and their inability to change it.
He had, in fact, changed his lot in life. He had founded
Gunman's Crossing, a place of legend, while keeping himself anonymous. Lawmen were no longer looking for him
because long ago he had stopped leading a gang and had
taken up permanent residence in the Crossing. From time
to time, when he started feeling closed in, he'd leave and
go to Denver for a few days, have himself a high old time,

and then return. And always, upon his return, he felt like he was coming home.

So if Gunman's Crossing still felt like home to him, why change things?

THIRTY-SIX

The saloon was called The Canyon, and it was not the one the piano music was coming from. It was, however, full to the rafters with armed men in various stages of drunkenness. As Clint, Heck, and McNab entered several men slapped them on the back and welcomed them.

"I'm glad they're all so happy," Clint said to Heck as they reached the bar.

"Me, too."

"What?" McNab asked.

"I said, do you want a beer?"

McNab nodded. Clint and Heck simultaneously decided to keep the kid between them. That way he could hear what they said, and they could keep him out of trouble. Already they could see someone at the other end of the bar was eyeing him, as if wondering what somebody so young was doing in the saloon—or in town.

"Three beers," Heck told the bartender.

"Comin' up."

The barman set three mugs in front of them. It took only one sip to determine that they were lukewarm.

"Coulda warned ya," the man said. "Most folks around here drink whiskey."

153

"This is fine," Heck said. "At least it's wet."

"Ain't seen you fellas around here before."

"We're just passing through," Clint said.

"Got a price on your heads?" he asked. "A posse on your tail?"

"Let's just say some people would be very interested to find us here," Clint replied.

"So what'd ya do—"

"You ask too many questions," Heck said, cutting the man off.

"Sorry," the bartender said, putting his hands up, palms out, "comes with the job. Ya don't wanna answer questions, ya don't have to."

"Thanks."

The man backed away and went to the other end of the bar. There he exchanged words with the man who was eyeing McNab. Abruptly that man pushed away from the bar and started walking towards them.

"You want to do the talking, Heck?" Clint asked.

"Might as well."

The man was about forty, tall and rangy, wearing a well-used gun on his right hip. As he reached Heck he was still looking at McNab. Heck put his hand on the man's chest to stop him. Slowly the man moved his eyes to Heck's face.

"Can I help you?" Heck asked.

The man hesitated, then said, "My business is with the young fella, here."

"You got no business with him," Heck said.

"I think I know him from somewhere," the man said. He looked at McNab. "I know you from somewhere?"

"I don't know you from nowhere," McNab said.

"I swear—"

"You heard the man," Heck said. "He don't know you."

"Man? He ain't no man, he's a kid."

"Whatever he is," Heck said, "he don't know you. Move on."

Suddenly the man squared up on Heck.

"Who you talkin' to, friend?"

"I'm talkin' to you, friend," Heck said.

Clint moved away from the bar so the man could see him clearly. The man seemed to realize he was facing three guns, and he backed off a bit.

"The name's Judson," he said.

"Nobody asked," Heck replied.

The man smiled.

"I'll be seein' you."

With that he turned and walked back to his space at the bar, which despite the crowded conditions had not filled up.

"That was a test," Clint said.

"Felt like it," Heck said.

"A test for what?" McNab asked.

"To see if we'd jump," Clint said.

"And we didn't?"

"Right," Heck said.

"Who's he work for?" McNab asked.

"Probably whoever owns the town," Heck said. "They probably brace all strangers like that."

"We better finish these beers and move on," Clint said. "Heck, any sign of Sunday or his gang?"

"No," Heck said, "none."

"Then I suggest we go and find a saloon that's got cold beer," Clint said.

"Sounds good to me," Heck agreed.

They left their warm beers on the bar and walked outside, aware that their progress was followed all the way by the fella name Judson.

The bartender came over to Judson and said, "So?"

"Better send word to the boss."

"What about?"

"The one with the big mouth," Judson said, "he's got little pin holes in his shirt."

"So?"

"So what makes holes in a man's shirt, Ralph?" Judson asked.

Ralph looked blank, then said, "Oh . . . a badge?"

"That's right," Judson said, "A badge. We got us a lawman in town."

"A lawm—"

"Not so loud!" Judson hissed. "Just get word to Mr. Cannon and see what he wants me to do—and keep it quiet, or there'll be a stampede to kill a lawman."

Outside McNab asked, "So what are we gonna do when we see Frank Sunday, or one of his gang?"

"Well," Heck said, "Sunday or Arch Jackson will recognize me. I don't know about the rest of the gang."

"And when they do they'll start shootin'?" the kid asked.

"Probably not," Clint said. "Not right off, anyway. They'll want to see who Heck's with, and then figure out what they want to do, bushwack us or face us in the street."

"Why would they bushwack us?" McNab asked. "They outnumber us seven to three."

"Really?" Heck asked.

"They don't?"

"Clint and I were sorta figurin' we had them outnumbered."

THIRTY-SEVEN

When there was a knock on the door Victor Cannon said, "Come."

The door opened and a weasel named Wesley came in, hat in hand. Usually, when there was a message from one of the three saloons a man like this was sent with a message.

"Don't come all the way in," Canon warned. "I can already smell you from here. What is it?"

"Word from Dollar Bill's that there's a lawman in town, Mr. Cannon," Wesley said.

"Who saw him?"

"Judson."

"Alone?"

"Three men altogether."

"Wearing a badge?"

Wesley shook his head.

"Judson said he seen the holes in his shirt where he wore a badge before."

Could have been an ex-lawman, but it was worth checking out.

"Tell Judson to take some men and check it out."

"And if it's a real lawman?"

"Just tell him to come here and let me know himself."

"Yes, sir."

Cannon took out a silver dollar and flipped it across the room to the old rummy. Wesley may have been sixty-five and a drunk but he plucked that coin out of the air with a sure hand.

"Thank you, sir."

"Just go."

When the man was gone Cannon went to the door to open it and let the stink out. If there was actually a lawman in town, though, there was a lot worse stink to get rid of.

Word got back to the Dollar Bill quicker than if it had been sent on a wire.

"Check it out, the boss says," the bartender said to Judson. "Then let him know."

Judson turned around and scanned the room. He saw two men who worked for Cannon and waved them over. He told each of them to go and get two more men each and meet him in front of the saloon.

"What's it about, Jud?" Amos Tyler asked.

"When you get back here with the men I'll let you know," Judson said.

Judson walked out with them, then pulled over a wooden chair and sat down in front of the saloon to wait.

THIRTY-EIGHT

They found a larger saloon with more activity—girls, gaming tables, some private poker games. There was plenty of pushing and shoving going on, but no shooting.

"This town has calmed down some," Heck said. "Three shots fired every other minute when I was here last."

"Must be the new rules," McNab observed.

"Probably," Clint said. "We need to check out the last saloon. If we don't see Sunday and his gang there, or anywhere around town, then either they have hotel rooms and are in them, or we did beat them here."

"Third saloon's down the street," Heck said. "Let's go."

The third saloon, The Whiskey River, was a lot like the second, only even more so. This was the major gathering place in town. All the games were run by the house, there were no private tables.

"See 'em anywhere?" Clint asked.

"I'd know Sunday, and Arch Johnson on sight," Heck said. "Not the others. I don't see those two, though."

"We could check the hotel," McNab said, "see if they registered."

"Word would get around that we were asking questions," Heck said. "Let's just stay here awhile. The beer's cold, at least."

So they decided to kill some time there and wait and at least slake their thirst.

Dan Judson studied his six men for a moment before speaking. All were competent hands with a gun, but none had his speed and accuracy. They were good for odd jobs.

"We don't know who these three are," he said. "One's a kid, wears his gun low. The others are old hands at it. You can tell by the way they stand. But the fact is, we don't know who they are or what they want, and Mr. Cannon wants us to find out."

"How are we supposed to do that?" Amos Tyler asked.

"We're gonna ask 'em, Amos," Judson said. "We're gonna ask 'em."

Clint, Heck, and McNab were still in The Whiskey River saloon when Judson and his six men came through the bat-wing doors. They stood just inside while Judson scanned the crowd. His eyes finally came to rest on the three of them standing at the bar.

"He's back, and he brought friends," McNab said. "What's he got against me?"

"It ain't you he's interested in, kid," Heck said. "Least-ways, not just you."

"I guess we've been noticed," Clint said. "He's been sent to find out who we are and what we want."

"How do you know that?"

"We been to a lot of towns, Dave," Heck said, "seen a lot of men with that look."

"So what're they gonna do?" McNab asked. "Brace it right here in a crowded saloon?"

"That fella there in front," Heck said, "he probably just wants to talk to us."

"And the other six?"

"They're just there to back his play if there's trouble," Clint said, "but they don't look like gun hands to me. If he had trouble in mind I think he would have brought better help."

"He's just tryin' to intimidate us with numbers," Heck said. "Watch, they won't even come over here with him."

Just as Heck said that Judson broke away from the other six men and approached them.

"Wow," McNab said, "how'd you know?"

"This ain't our first time at the rodeo, kid," Heck said.

THIRTY-NINE

When Judson fronted them he locked eyes with Heck Thomas.

"Lawman," he said.

"I used to be," Heck said, without hesitation.

"You should get yourself some new shirts," Judson said. "Ones without the pin holes."

Heck touched the place on his shirt where his badge was usually pinned, then said to Judson, "Good point. Thanks."

"So what are you boys doin' in town?" Judson asked.

"Passin' through."

"Friend," Judson said, "nobody just passes through Gunman's Crossing."

"Well," Heck said, "we kinda found it by accident. Came in at the other end of town, actually."

"The other end?" Judson frowned. "You mean Old Town?"

"I guess that's what I mean," Heck said.

"How'd you get there?"

"Back way."

"There ain't no back way," Judson said.

"Well," Heck said, "we stumbled across one."

Judson looked unhappy. Clint had no doubt that the man had a boss he was going to have to give this news to.

"So you ain't on the run?" he asked.

"One of us might be," Heck said. "But we don't discuss it."

"What're your names?"

"Is this some sort of . . . official inquiry?" Clint asked.

"You could call it that," Judson said. "You could also call me and my friends the welcoming committee."

Clint looked past Judson to the six men who had fanned out from the door.

"They seem a bit nervous."

"They can get a might jittery," Judson said. "I got other men who ain't so nervous, though . . . if I need them."

"You ain't gonna need them," Heck said. "We just need to stay here a day or two. If you got some rules we need to know about—"

"The only rule here is you answer questions," Judson said, "and if you run into any trouble you handle it yourself."

"Sounds fair."

"So I'll need those names."

Heck gave the man three names so quickly off the top of his head Clint wasn't sure he'd even remember them later. Actually, he concocted names for himself and Clint, but gave Dave McNab's real name.

"Where you boys stayin'?" Judson asked.

"That hotel in . . . what'd you call it . . . Old Town?"

"That dump?" the man said. "We got much nicer hotels you could stay in."

"That one's . . . quiet," Heck said.

"Well, it is that," Judson said. "That end of town is totally dead except for that fool who runs the hotel."

"We figure we might stay out of trouble that way," Clint said.

"Doesn't seem to me you boys worry much about stayin' out of trouble," Judson said.

"We try," Clint said.

"Well," Judson said, "enjoy your drinks, and your couple of days here. I'm sure we'll be talkin' again."

"We look forward to it," Heck said.

Judson nodded, backed away. Only when he was in the midst of his men did he turn and walk to the batwing doors.

"What the hell—" McNab exploded.

"What's the matter, boy?" Heck asked.

"You gave him my real name."

"He woulda recognized our names," Heck said. "They don't know you from Adams."

"Well . . ." McNab said.

"Don't fret, Dave," Clint said. "Come on, I'll buy you another beer, and then we can go back to the hotel."

"But . . . I thought I'd play some poker."

"You any good at it?" Clint asked.

"Good enough."

"Enough for what?" Clint asked. "Look, did you hear what we told that fella about staying out of trouble?"

"Yeah, so—"

"We meant it," Clint said. "It looks like we got here before Frank Sunday and his gang. Now we need to stay out of trouble and be on the lookout for them."

"How we gonna do that from the hotel?"

"Same way we do it when we camp," Heck said. "We'll take split watches. Clint, I'll take the first, you take the second."

"What about me?" McNab asked.

"You drink your beer and then turn in," Clint said. "Somebody has to be fresh in the morning."

"You're not lettin' me stand watch because you think I'll get into trouble."

Clint and Heck exchanged a glance and then Heck slapped the young man on the back and said, "Son, you got that exactly right."

FORTY

This time Dan Judson reported to Victor Cannon himself.

"What names did they give you?" Cannon asked.

"Hendricks, Carter, and McNab."

Cannon frowned.

"I never heard of any of them."

"Me, neither."

"They're probably lying," Cannon said, rubbing his chin. "Most men lie about their names, here."

"So you don't think he's an ex-lawman?" Judson asked. "A real lawman would never step foot in this town."

"I guess that would depend on who he was after," Cannon said, "and how bad he wanted him. "Do you have anyone in town right now who's got a high price on his head? A big reputation?"

"Nobody like that," Judson said. "The town is full of small-timers, right now."

"So what would bring these three men here?"

"I don't know."

"I do."

"What?"

"Somebody who's not here yet," Cannon said. "Somebody who's on his way. Somehow, these three found out and they got here first."

"So some big rep is comin' in the next two days?"

"Probably," Cannon said. "Look, I want somebody to look into this back way these fellas talked about. I thought this town was pretty well boxed in. If there's another way in I want it covered from now on."

"I'll have it checked out."

"Make sure you send somebody you trust," Cannon said. "Don't send an idiot."

"Yes, sir."

"And have somebody keep an eye on these three," Cannon said. "Especially if they split up."

"Right."

"Go ahead," Cannon said. "Take care of it."

"Yes, sir."

Judson headed for the door but Cannon stopped him.

"Jud!"

"Yeah?"

"You got anybody in town right now who can use a gun?" the man asked. "I mean, really handle a gun."

"Yeah," Judson said. "Me, and a couple of other good boys. Murch and Jessup."

"Okay," Cannon said, "keep them available. We just might need them."

"Yes, sir."

Judson left and Victor Cannon sat back in his chair to ponder the situation. Three strangers, one likely a lawman, and if one was likely, then probably all three. All he'd have to do was start a rumor that they were law and the small-timers in town would be fighting to take them down. Still it'd be interesting to know who they were, and who they were waiting for.

FORTY-ONE

Clint had the second watch, which meant he was awake when Frank Sunday and his gang rode into Gunman's Crossing.

Of course, he didn't know for sure it was the Sunday gang, but seven men riding in together was a pretty good indication. Also, Heck had described both Sunday and Arch Jackson, and the fearsome countenance they presented together. Clint didn't know if there were two other such men as these two riding down the main street right now, with five others grouped behind them.

It had to be them.

Sunday had insisted they camp just outside of Gunman's Crossing and ride in early in the morning, in daylight.

"You never know what you're gonna run into," he told his men, "especially in that town."

So they rode in at first light, when most of the denizens of the town—and its visitors—were still sawing wood. They only saw one man, seated on a chair in front of The Whiskey River saloon. Sunday figured it was maybe a drunk—desperate for his first drink of the day.

They all rode past the man, ignoring him.

• • •

Clint had not chosen the position in front of the saloon to keep watch from. That decision had been made by Heck Thomas, and it had been a good one. It afforded one a view of the entire street.

His first instinct was to hurry back to the hotel to get Heck and McNab, but he held himself in check until the seven men had ridden past him. But he still couldn't hurry to the hotel because he'd have to pass the livery on the way. He stood up at one point, ready to leave his post, then sat back down and realized the wisdom of remaining where he was. From this vantage point he'd be able to see where the gang decided to stay. He settled back in his chair, slouched, and tried to look like someone sitting in front of the saloon, impatiently waiting for his first drink of the day.

Frank Sunday, Arch Jackson, and the gang unsaddled their horses and put them in stalls. It was early, and the livery—one of several in town—had been open. It was something Sunday remembered about the Crossing. No locked doors. Anyone caught stealing in the Crossing would be in a lot of trouble. You could kill somebody in town and get away with it, but try stealing and that was another story.

There were eight empty stalls in the large livery, and they filled seven of them.

"This is a good sign," Sunday told Jackson. "Won't be that many visitors in town."

"How much of a population has this place got?" Jackson asked.

"A lot more than it used to."

"I thought it was just a glorified hideout."

"Yeah," Sunday said, with a nod, "it used to be."

They unsaddled their horses, then grabbed their saddle-bags and rifles and left the livery.

"Let's not stay in the same places," he announced. "Split up, no more than two or three per hotel or boarding house. No point in bunching up and looking for trouble."

They all agreed, and started walking back to the center of town.

Clint saw the men walking with their saddlebags and rifles. For just a moment he thought he could be in a lot of trouble if they came for him. Seven against one was heavy odds for anyone, even him. But they had no reason to come for him, or even approach him. They split up and he watched as the two big men, Sunday and Jackson, went to the same hotel. The rest of the gang continued walking until two went into one of the other hotels. The other three men kept going, and Clint assumed they were heading for one of the town's boarding houses—or maybe even one of the cat houses.

When the street was empty he got up and headed for his hotel.

He woke Heck first, then they woke McNab.

"How are we gonna do this?" McNab asked, as they hurried down the stairs to the lobby.

"Clint knows where Sunday and Jackson are stayin'," Heck said. "We'll have to take them first. Without their boss the other five will be easier."

"Other five?" McNab asked. "If we get Sunday and Jackson why do we need the others?"

"Because they're all killers," Heck said. He stopped walking, turned and stared at the kid. "I don't do my job halfway, son. I came here for the whole Sunday gang, and I intend to get 'em."

"And what about all these others fellas in town?" McNab asked. "They just gonna let us take 'em?"

"Sure they are," Heck said. "Why not? They'll all just mind their business."

"What about when they find out you're a lawman?"

"Well," Heck said, "we're gonna try not to let them find out."

FORTY-TWO

Clint, Heck, and McNab entered the hotel Clint had seen both Sunday and Jackson go into. He'd described the two men to Heck, who said he was sure that was them.

"Help you gents?" the desk clerk asked.

"Thanks," Heck said, reaching for the register, "we'll just help ourselves."

He opened the book and found the names "Frank Sunday" and "Arch Jackson."

"Didn't even bother to use phony names," he said, slamming the book closed. "They got separate rooms."

"We should split up," Clint said.

"The kid and I will take Frank," Heck said. "He's in room six. You take Arch Jackson in seven."

"What about the fellas outside?" Clint asked.

"What fellas?" McNab asked.

"We've been watched since last night," Heck explained.

"I ain't seen nobody."

"Clint and I saw them."

"What were they doin'?"

"Just watchin' us, kid," Heck said. "Just watchin'—and I think that's all they'll do."

• • •

Across the street Dan Judson came up on his two men,
Murch and Jessup, to whom he had given the task of keeping an eye on the three strangers.

"What do we got?" he asked.

"They're inside the hotel," Murch said.

"And?"

"And we saw Frank Sunday and his gang ride in."

"Sunday! That's who they're waitin' for. Who's stayin'
at that hotel?" Judson asked.

"Sunday and Arch Jackson."

"And the rest of the gang?"

"Split up," Jessup said. "Stayin' different places."

"So they're goin' for Sunday and Jackson first."

"Looks like it," Murch said.

"There's somethin' else," Jessup said.

"What's that?"

"I recognized one of the men," Jessup said. "Seen him
before once, in San Antonio."

"Oh yeah? Which one?"

"The taller one," Jessup said. "Dan, it's Clint Adams."

"The Gunsmith?"

"One and the same."

"Jesus."

"What do we do?" Murch asked. "Go in?"

"No," Dan Judson said. "Let's wait out here and see how
it plays out."

"So we're just gonna watch?" Murch asked.

"We're just gonna watch . . . for now."

Frank Sunday dropped his gear on his bed and decided he
needed a drink now. He left his room and walked across the
hall and down a few doors to Arch Jackson's, who let him
in after he knocked.

"I'm headin' for the saloon," Sunday said. "You
comin'?"

"Sure," Jackson said, "but what about checkin' in with Victor Cannon? He's gonna wanna know we're here."

"Yeah, we'll go and see him after we wash some of this trail dust out of our throats." Jackson reached to take his rifle off the bed but Sunday said, "Leave it, Arch. We ain't gonna need rifles."

Jackson hesitated and was drawing his hand away from the weapon just as the door to the room flew open.

At the top of the stairs Heck Thomas said, "We'll just kick the doors in and take 'em before they know what's goin' on."

"Okay," Clint said.

They moved down the hall and reached Sunday's room first. Heck and McNab stopped, waited until Clint reached Arch Jackson's door. Then Heck and Clint both lifted their legs and kicked. The doors to the respective rooms slammed open. As soon as Heck and McNab entered the room and found it empty the marshal knew his friend was in trouble.

Clint kicked the door open and stepped into the doorway. He saw the two big men turn their heads towards him, surprised at his entry, but he was just as surprised to see two men in the room instead of one.

They all went for their guns.

Frank Sunday and Arch Jackson didn't know who the man was, but that didn't matter to them. They drew their guns and started shooting.

Clint's first shot took Jackson high in the chest on the right side, but seemed to have no effect on the big man. At that point he had to duck out of the room because both men were firing as fast as they could.

Chunks of wood were gouged out of the door jamb and the hallway wall as Heck and McNab hurried down the hall to assist Clint.

Meanwhile, inside the room Sunday yelled to Jackson, "The window!"

Then the shooting stopped and there was the sound of breaking glass.

FORTY-THREE

"Downstairs!" Clint shouted.

"What?" McNab asked.

"That was the window!"

McNab looked puzzled but Heck Thomas understood. He took off down the hall and hurried down the stairs to the lobby with Clint close behind him. McNab lagged behind.

As Heck and Clint ran through the lobby Frank Sunday and Arch Jackson were getting to their feet. Jackson was bleeding from the bullet wound in his shoulder, but it didn't seem to slow him down. He had dropped his gun when he hit the ground and instead of looking for it he ran straight at Heck and Clint as they came out onto the street.

The big man slammed into both of them, driving them back and to the ground. Surprised, both men nonetheless managed to hold onto their guns. But Jackson wasn't done. He swung and hit Heck in the face with a backhanded blow that felt like a sledgehammer. The marshal's head swam as he fell to the ground again, wondering if his jaw was broken.

Clint got to his knees just as Arch Jackson turned his attention back to him. The man lunged for him, but Clint managed to scoot away, out of his reach.

While this was going on Frank Sunday, who had also lost his gun when he hit the ground, frantically began searching for it. Finally he spotted it and rushed to pick it up. At that moment Dave McNab came running out into the street. He stopped short and took in the scene. To his left Clint, Heck, and Arch Jackson were still on the ground. To his right Frank Sunday was scrambling for his gun.

McNab turned his attention to the gang leader.

Clint brought his gun around, intending to club Arch Jackson with it, but suddenly a big hand closed over his hand and his gun. Jackson squeezed and the pain made Clint gasp. He fought to hold onto the gun, knowing that if he let the man pull it from his hand he'd use his own gun against him. But the bigger man's superior strength began to exert itself and he was losing his hold on the weapon. Desperately he kicked out and caught Jackson in the groin. The man grunted, but held on. Clint kicked again and this time the man's grip lessened. He managed to pull his gun free from Jackson just as Heck rose up and brought his gun down on the back of the big man's head. Jackson grunted again, turned on Heck, but Clint scrambled forward and slammed his gun into the man's head in the same spot. All of the fight went out of the hulking brute and he fell to the ground on his face.

Clint and Heck turned to look at Frank Sunday and saw that McNab was between them and the gang leader.

"Dave!" Clint shouted.

But McNab didn't hear him. He and Frank Sunday were frozen in their own tableau . . .

Frank Sunday reached for his gun and stopped when he saw the kid standing there.

"Go ahead, Sunday," McNab said. "Pick it up. Holster it. I'll give you a chance."

"You're crazy, kid," Sunday said. "I'll kill you."

McNab smiled.

"You'll try."

Sunday grinned and reached for the gun.

"Two fingers," McNab said. "Holster it. Let's make this fair."

"Fair," Sunday said. "Sure, kid."

Sunday picked his gun up from the dirt with two fingers and slid it into his holster.

"Can I get up?" he asked.

"Sure," McNab said. "Like I said. This is gonna be fair."

Sunday got to his feet. Beyond McNab he saw Clint and Heck Thomas watching.

"What about your friends?" he asked.

"They won't interfere," McNab said.

It was true. Clint had gotten to his feet with intentions of stopping the showdown, but Heck had put his hand on Clint's arm.

"Let him go, Clint," Heck said. "He's gonna have to do it sometime."

Sunday decided to concentrate on the kid in front of him. Once he killed him he could worry about Marshal Heck Thomas and the other one, meanwhile, maybe his men would hear the commotion and come running.

"Okay, kid," Sunday said. "Go ahead."

"After you, Mr. Sunday."

"Mr. Sunday," the gang leader said. "I like that."

Sunday went for his gun, his move swift and confident, but before he could even clear leather Dave McNab drew, fired . . . and holstered his weapon, again.

His bullet hit Frank Sunday in the chest and punctured his heart. The man fell flat onto his face.

"Jesus," Heck Thomas said. "Did you see that?"

"Barely," Clint said, impressed. He didn't think he'd ever seen a faster move.

McNab turned and looked at them. Between them on the ground Arch Jackson rolled over and groaned. Then all three of them looked at the three men watching from across the street. They'd been joined by others who had come out of the saloons when the shooting started. Clint and Heck figured Sunday's gang must be among them, but nobody was moving to do anything but watch.

Above them, standing in the window of his office, Victor Cannon had watched the whole thing. Dan Judson looked up at Cannon for instructions. His boss simply shook his head.

"Come on," Judson said to his two men.

"What—" Murch started.

"It's all over here," Judson said. "Let's go."

He turned and walked away, his two puzzled men following him. The others stayed where they were, sensing that there was more to come.

In his office Victor Cannon stared down. Of the three men it was obvious which one was the Gunsmith. When Judson told him he'd identified at least one of the men as Clint Adams Cannon had said, "Just watch him. Maybe they'll do what they came to do and leave."

"But what—"

"Do you want to face the Gunsmith, Jud?"

"Well . . . no."

"Neither do I," Cannon said. "We got a good thing here. Let's not ruin it."

"Okay, Boss."

Now, after seeing the speed with which the young man had killed Frank Sunday he knew he'd made the right decision. He assumed the third man would be at least as good with a gun as Clint Adams and the kid. They could do a lot of damage if pushed.

Just go, he thought. Just go . . .

"What's that about?" Heck asked aloud.

"I don't know," Clint said. He looked up and saw the

man in the window. "I think we just got a free pass."

"But why?"

"That I don't know." He looked at Heck. "What about the rest of the gang?"

Heck took a moment to think it over. His eyes raked over the crowd of men still watching.

"Let's forget it. Without Sunday they'll disband."

"You want to take Jackson all the way back to Oklahoma Territory?" Clint asked.

"I don't want to, but . . ."

McNab came walking over and grinned at the two of them.

"Why take him back?" he asked, and before they could react McNab drew and shot the man through the head.

"What the hell—" Heck said.

McNab holstered his gun and backed away.

"Got a problem with that?" he asked.

Suddenly, Dave McNab looked a lot older than he had before. The look on his face was confident and not in the least innocent.

"What's going on, Dave?" Clint asked.

"You don't think I came along just to help, do you?" he asked.

"I guess not."

"Which one of us do you want, kid?" Heck asked.

McNab pointed at Clint and said, "Him." He looked at Clint. "I wanted you to see what I could do to somebody like Frank Sunday."

"I saw."

"Impressed?"

"Oh, yeah."

"So now it's you and me," McNab said. He looked at Heck, again. "I know I plugged that poker chip back in Tucumcari."

"Yeah, you did."

"After I kill him, I'm gonna kill you, Marshal."

"Kid," Heck said, "after seein' your move I don't doubt you could kill me."

"Smart man."

"But I don't have to worry about that."

"Why not?"

"'Cause you ain't gonna get past Clint."

"Says you."

"I'm tellin' you, kid," Heck said. "You can't beat him. He's the Gunsmith."

"I know who he is," McNab said, "and I can beat him."

"Fine," Heck said. "Find out the hard way."

"Move off the street, Heck," Clint said.

Heck took one last look down at Arch Jackson, then joined the men watching from the boardwalk. There was some quick wagering going on and he got a piece of it. Might as well make some money before they left town. He knew there was a danger that Sunday's men might pass the word he was a lawman, but it seemed they were content to stay hidden and watch with their mouths shut.

He turned his attention to the street . . .

"You got your rep, kid," Clint said. "You killed Frank Sunday. You can leave here with that."

"Frank Sunday was nothin'," McNab said. "Once I kill you, then I'll have me a name."

"Kid—"

"No more talkin', Adams!" McNab snapped.

Clint sighed. He probably could have saved himself a lot of trouble if he'd just killed McNab back in Tucumcari, with his friends.

McNab backed away and Clint stood his ground. The kid spread his feet and flexed his hand while Clint stood very still. The crowd held its breath—including Heck Thomas. He'd witnessed the kid's move, and he didn't think he'd ever seen a faster one.

Except, he thought, as Clint Adams cleanly outdrew
Dave McNab and killed him, for the Gunsmith's.

Clint walked over to where Heck Thomas was collecting
money.

"You ready to go?" he asked.

Heck grabbed the last dollar and said, "If you are."

The crowd was quiet, stunned by the speed of Clint
Adams's draw. After seeing McNab kill Frank Sunday
very few of them thought that Clint could beat him. Of
course, very few of them knew who he really was.

As they walked back to Old Town to collect their horses
Clint asked, "You weren't worried, were you?"

"Me?" Heck asked. "Naw. I bet on you, didn't I?"

Watch for

ALIVE OR NOTHING

292nd novel in the exciting GUNSMITH series
from Jove

Coming in April!

J. R. ROBERTS

THE GUNSMITH

GIANT-SIZED ADVENTURE FROM AVENGING ANGEL LONGARM.

LONGARM AND THE DEADLY DEAD MAN
0-515-13547-X

THIS ALL-NEW, GIANT-SIZED ADVENTURE IN THE
POPULAR ALL-ACTION SERIES PUTS THE "WILD"
BACK IN THE WILD WEST—AND PROVES THAT A
DEAD OUTLAW IS SAFER IN HIS GRAVE THAN
FACING AN AVENGING ANGEL NAMED LONGARM.

LONGARM AND THE BARTERED BRIDES
0-515-13834-7

SOME MEN, ACHING FOR FEMALE COMPANIONSHIP,
HAVE SENT AWAY FOR BRIDES. BUT WHEN THE
WOMENFOLK NEVER SHOW, THESE HOMBRES HIRE
ON GUNSLINGER CUSTIS LONG TO DO WHAT HE
DOES SECOND-BEST: SKIRT-CHASING.

LONGARM

**Explore the exciting Old West with one
of the men who made it wild!**